CROSSING OVER AT REMAGEN

A SOLDIER'S JOURNEY

Michael Klein

DEDICATION

To my father who was the inspiration for this story:
PFC Corstian Klein
311th Infantry Regiment
78th Infantry Division aka "The Lightning Division"

CONTENTS

Acknowledgments   i

Introduction   iii

1 Kalenborn   7

2 Mike Company   19

3 Zero Three Thirty Hours   34

4 The Attack   44

5 Meckenheim   53

6 Remagen   62

7 The Bridge   71

8 Erpel   83

9 Unkel   92

10 Scheuren   100

11 The March   112

12 Bad Honnef   121

13 Werwolf   130

14 Ittenbach   139

Appendix   150

ACKNOWLEDGMENTS

I would like to start by thanking my father, as he is the inspiration for this book. My father did not like talking about what he experienced during the war, so for many years, I did not think that this was a book that I would ever be able to write. But as I researched the Battle of Remagen, I was able to piece together a story based on the facts of that battle. I then interspersed that story with some of the more mundane facts about the war that my father shared with me.

My research was pretty limited because there isn't a lot written about the Battle of Remagen. However, it began for me when I read my father's combat journal, "Combat Journal, The Story of the Timberwolf Regiment of the 78th Lighting Division in World War II, 1944-1945." I would like to thank the men of the 311th Infantry Regiment who worked so hard to put together a history of what my father's unit accomplished during World War II. That Combat Journal was an invaluable resource for me in writing this book.

I would also like to thank Ken Hechler, for his excellent book, "The Bridge at Remagen." This was a great resource for me and helped me to understand the broader picture of what was accomplished by my father and the men he fought alongside during this pivotal moment in the war.

Many of the stories in this book have been taken from the experiences I had while serving in the Army. I would like to thank the men of the 286th Combat Engineer Company for their service and for giving me a shared experience that allowed me to talk to my father about his time in the military. Through this shared experience,

I was able to hear stories from my father that I otherwise would not have heard. I honestly believe that without the experience of serving in a combat unit my father would not have shared with me many of the stories that made this book possible.

Lastly, I would like to thank my family for supporting me in this venture. Their encouragement and motivation were instrumental in making this labor of love possible. Without them, this tribute to my father would have remained a vague notion and would never have come to fruition. I would especially like to thank my loving wife Rebecca. It was her patience and encouragement that made this tribute to my father and the people with whom he served a reality.

INTRODUCTION

The purpose of the book is to honor the sacrifices made by my father as he served his country in the Second World War. I have always been proud of my father's service and I hope this book will help the reader appreciate the sacrifices made by otherwise ordinary citizens when they were called to serve.

The main character of Gerrit Jansen is based on my father. And many of the experiences of Jansen are based on stories my father told me about his experiences during the war. Generally, Jansen's actions and demeanor are based on my father. The other characters of the story are based partly on men my father served with or on my experiences of serving in the military.

I wanted to write this book mainly to honor my father and his memory, but also to hopefully shed some light on an important battle in World War II that most people have never even heard about and a battle that has been largely forgotten, even by history buffs.

The Battle of Remagen was a clear example of an engagement between the Americans and the Germans in which the luck consistently broke in favor of the Americans. The loss of the bridge and the subsequent battle convinced many Germans that God Himself had sided against the German Army in contradiction to the phrase "Gott mit uns" (God with us) which was printed on their belt buckles. The Battle of Remagen was not a turning point of the war, but most historians believe that it was an important and decisive battle that did significantly shorten the war in Europe.

Hopefully, this will give the reader a glimpse into the daily lives of ordinary men who were called upon to do extraordinary things. That is what I think about when I think about my father.

My father never spoke to me specifically about his experiences in combat. This is the reason that this book is written as historical fiction. I have done my best to portray as many facts as accurately as possible, but I felt that writing a fictional account gave me the latitude to make minor changes and include other fictional details to make a more readable story.

I hope that this book works as a tribute to my father and to the men of his regiment who fought and died for their country. I also hope that it will help shine a spotlight on the Battle of Remagen, a forgotten piece of American history. It is my desire that, in writing this novel, I will have succeeded on both accounts in the eyes of the reader.

CHAPTER ONE

KALENBORN

March 7, 1945
0840 Hours

Several GIs were standing around the outside of a medical tent, stamping their feet and rubbing their hands to stay warm in the chilly morning air of Kalenborn, Germany on Wednesday, the 7th of March 1945. Their breath, visible in the muted morning light, turned into a slight puff of steam as it hit the cool air. Some men were smoking and expelling huge clouds of cigarette smoke that mixed with their breath as they waited for treatment.

Most of the GIs were waiting to see the medic for the same reason. Having just come off a break in the fighting, some had used some of their spare time to spend a few hours with some of the local women. Those men were now questioning their decision-making processes and regretting their choices of female companionship. The conversations that could be heard were generally either complaining about or specifically avoiding the subject of sex and the local female population.

A gray overcast sky made the morning seem even colder, but as most of the combat veterans knew, those same clouds would make their nights sleeping outside a little bit warmer. In the latter part of the winter of 1945, being cold, tired, and wet, was a normal condition for the men of the 311th Infantry Regiment.

The soldiers were separated into tight little groups as they waited outside the aid tent, with the Replacements and the Veterans clearly separated. The Replacements had only been in theater for a couple of weeks. At this point in the war, most of the Veterans had seen too many of these green new soldiers die. Becoming emotionally attached to a Replacement usually meant pain later as you watched the life drain out of a face that was young and full of promise. So, to avoid this, the Veterans kept a physical and emotional distance between themselves and the new troops.

Jansen came to his unit as a Replacement a couple of weeks ago. He was off by himself leaning up against a jeep, smoking a cigarette. His hand was covered with a field dressing. All things considered; Jansen was enjoying his time away from his unit. Sure, he was cold and tired, but there was a break in the combat, and anytime in the Army when you are not being told what to do was enjoyable.

Jansen was staring off into the distance looking at nothing in particular when he noticed that an officer was entering the area. His body immediately tensed a little as he readied himself to come to attention and salute his superior.

The officer Jansen noticed was a chaplain, who then walked into the group of soldiers. This chaplain was probably in his late 20s, young for a clergyman and chaplain, but much older than most of the soldiers in the group the young minister has just infiltrated. The chaplain had a face that made him seem younger and at the same time older than the men whom he was currently called to minister. There was a pearl of calm wisdom in his eyes that fostered this perception.

Most of the men ignored him as if making eye contact with a man of the cloth would cause them to burst into flames for the sins they so recently had committed. They knew why they were there, and they did not want to be reminded of the moral and practical implications of their actions.

Jansen was the only man who came to attention and saluted the officer. The chaplain returned the salute and walked over to Jansen since he was the only man that seemed even remotely interested in talking to a member of the clergy. Or to be honest, the only man that even acknowledged his presence.

"Good morning soldier, I'm Chaplain Martin. Where are you from?"

"South Dakota, sir," replied Jansen rather stiffly.

"At ease soldier, contrary to popular opinion, it isn't a Chaplain's job to make people feel uncomfortable. Tell me if I'm wrong, but there is enough discomfort in your life right now? Relax, what's your name?"

"Garret, sir."

"Oh, and that's another thing, please don't call me sir. You can call me Pastor Luke, or Chaplain Martin if calling me Pastor Luke is a little too informal for you. I understand that different religious traditions have specific views on how to address the clergy."

"I'd prefer Chaplain Martin if that is okay with you," replied Jansen.

Chaplain Martin could see that Jansen was becoming less rigid and beginning to relax a little. Martin knew that it was a good sign. Too often the soldiers to whom he was trying to minister were too uncomfortable and never really let their guard down around him, either because they were uneasy around officers, or because they felt weird talking to a pastor, or both. But with Garret, things were not like that, and given what everyone in this unit had been through, Martin held out hope for reaching this young kid from South Dakota.

"That is totally fine. How long have you been in-country Garret?" Chaplain Martin asked.

Garret returned to leaning up against the jeep. He liked this pastor. He reminded Garret of one of the simple country pastors he knew growing up in South Dakota. Country pastors were less assuming and conventional than their big-city counterparts. But that is not to say that these seemingly humble pastors were dumb or did not know anything. Garret could remember many Sunday potlucks, listening to his pastor discussing some minor point of theology with some of the Elders of his church. As he grew older, even though he only had an 8th-grade education, Jansen even found the temerity to interject comments or even pointed questions into those debates.

Garret's mind quickly returned to the conversation at hand, "I've only been with the 311th for a couple of weeks Chaplain Martin."

"That explains why I don't recognize you. I make it a point to try to get to know as many of the men as possible. But with the Replacements, it is hard since I haven't had as much time with them. Did you attend services back home?"

"Yeah, my dad was a stickler for going to church every Sunday. He was insistent on observing the Sabbath. That meant coming home after services, and just relaxing the rest of the day," Garret replied. "It doesn't always work out that way in combat though."

Garret's voice trailed off. He was letting his guard down, now he was in danger of letting his mind dwell on the aspects of combat that he would rather not think about. Chaplain Martin could sense what was going on in Garret's head and quickly brought the conversation back to a subject that would put the young soldier's mind at ease.

"We have a great bunch of men in the chaplain's staff, and we honestly do our best to minister to every man in this regiment, whether they come to services or not. We are still hoping that we will be able to have a service for each of the battalions this Sunday if the schedule allows. What battalion are you in?"

"I'm in the Third Battalion, Chaplain," answered Garret.

"If we can have Chapel this Sunday, I'll see if I can put in for duty with the Third Battalion. If not, then I know for a fact that one of the other chaplains will do an excellent job."

Then Martin put his hand on Garret's shoulder and softened his voice, "Listen, Garret, I know that it is hard for you right now. Some of the Veterans may think that you have nothing to complain about because you haven't been through as much as they have. They think that because they have been with this unit since it first arrived in-country they have had a harder time than you. But you and I know that just isn't true. What those Veterans don't know is how hard it is to adjust to life in a forward area at first. And for you Replacements, it's even harder because you are seen as outsiders. I know because I've talked to enough Replacements and have heard the same story many times. So, Garret, I just want you to know that I will always be available if you need anything. The Chaplain's staff is praying for you boys around the clock. God brought you to this time and place for a purpose, and He will be with you no matter what."

Garret let out a heavy sigh as he fought back his emotions. He knew that there was a reason he liked this chaplain. A calmness came over him as he looked at Chaplain Martin. There was a short moment of silence then Garret said, "Thank you, chaplain. I really mean that. It has been hard, and I've seen more than I care to remember. Thank you for reminding me that, no matter what, I am not in this alone."

"You are very welcome. I've enjoyed talking to you. I will keep you in my prayers. Have you ever been given one of the Army's pocket Bibles? I have one I could give you if you want."

"No Chaplain Martin, I haven't. I have a regular Bible, but it is too big to take in the field, so I usually don't have it with me," Garret replied.

"Well here you go Garret," Chaplain Martin reached into his coat and pulled out a new pocket-sized Bible, and handed it to Garret. "Oh, and by the way, do you think any of these other guys would want to talk to a chaplain or maybe might want a Bible, I have a couple more that I could give out?"

"You could try Chaplain Martin, but something tells me that these guys are preoccupied with something other than spiritual matters at the moment," joked Garret.

"Well, I'll quit while I'm ahead then. May God bless you and keep you, Garret. Take care, I'll be praying for you," the chaplain said as he left the area, pleased that he was able to reach at least one of the souls from the Regiment he was called to serve.

Garret Jansen finally returned to smoking his cigarette, feeling as well he had in days. Grateful for the time to connect with Chaplain Martin and comforted to feel a connection to his faith and his family back home.

Jansen sat looking out at the cluster of tents that made up this part of the Regimental Headquarters. There were trucks, jeeps, and the occasional tank or half-track moving in and out of the area. This area was mainly just for the grunts though. The officers and higher-ranking support staff were most likely holed up in some fancy house or hotel, sleeping on real beds and eating warm meals.

With all that he had been through in the last few weeks, Jansen appreciated having quiet moments to himself. At home growing up in a large family, he would sometimes wake up in the middle of the night and go off to some unoccupied area of the house and read. This was the only time that he could be alone, and he felt that it gave him time to think. Now, being alone with his thoughts was a luxury that he did not get to enjoy very often.

And then, almost on cue, he saw a young soldier walking toward him. The kid was short and skinny and looked like he was barely old enough to wear the uniform. But he did look vaguely familiar. The young soldier walked over to Jansen.

"Hey buddy, you look familiar," said the Replacement.

Jansen replied, "Yeah, I think we were on the same truck when we were sent to our units a couple of weeks ago."

"My name is Tailor, how are you holding up?"

"As well as can be expected," Jansen replied.

In the short time that Jansen had been in-country, he had already seen his share of the dead and wounded. It had been rough on him, and his way of dealing with it had been to focus on the moment or task at hand. He tried not to dwell on things in the past that he could not change. Jansen was worried that Tailor would be the type that wanted to talk about the horrible things they had seen in the short amount of time since they had come to the European Theater of Operations, or the ETO, as the Army called it. That was the last thing that Jansen wanted right now after talking to the chaplain. He was feeling relaxed and peaceful for the first time in a long time. And he did not want to talk to some kid who might say something stupid and ruin Jansen's good mood. But in order to steer the conversation where he wanted it to go, he decided to get this kid talking about life back home.

"So, Tailor, do you have a first name?"

"Yeah, it's Ron," Tailor replied.

"Mine's Garret, Garret Jansen. Where are you from?" Jansen responded, trying to keep the conversation light.

"I'm from Missouri, how 'bout you?"

"I'm from a boring little farm town in South Dakota that nobody has ever heard of," Jansen was trying to end the conversation before it veered into talking about life in combat.

"Yeah, I know what you mean, my hometown is pretty boring too. I don't think that anyone who hasn't lived there would know the name of my town either. My town doesn't even have a movie theater."

Tailor mentioning a movie theater meant almost nothing to Jansen. Having grown up on a farm in South Dakota during the Depression, Jansen's family was the epitome of "dirt poor." His family had neither the time nor the money to spend (or as Jansen's dad would say "waste") on things like movies. So naturally, he had never been to the movies. The closest Jansen ever came to seeing a movie was watching training films in basic training when he had first joined the Army.

"I know what you mean, a big night for me back home was riding into town with my brother to buy shotgun shells so we could spend the weekend shooting birds on my dad's farm," Jansen replied.

A calm look came over Tailor's face, "You know I didn't think much of it growing up in Missouri, but man I sure miss home now."

Then the expression on Tailor's face quickly changed again, and it was clear that he was now contrasting his life in Missouri to what he had seen in his short time in Germany. "This place is definitely not Missouri," he said with a slight crack in his voice.

Jansen could see that this conversation was about to take a turn into an area he did not want it to go. Almost as if by Divine Providence a medic standing outside the tent yelled out, "Jansen, Private Jansen."

"That's me, nice talking to you, Tailor. Stay safe. I'm sure we'll both be back in our boring towns before we know it," Jansen said in a voice that sounded a little relieved.

Jansen's words and his hopeful tone snapped Tailor's mind back to the present, "Hey, nice talking to you too Jansen. Keep your head down. I'm sure we'll see each other again when all this is over."

Jansen, thankful that he had dodged a metaphorical bullet, weaved his way through the other soldiers on his way to the entrance of the tent. Jansen walked up to the medic who had called his name and announced, "I'm Jansen."

"Come with me private," came a reply from the obviously irritated medic who had been working all morning without a break.

The two soldiers made their way into the tent, it was a little warmer in the tent than it was outside, but not by much. The two men walked behind a screen and the medic ordered Jansen to drop his pants.

"Excuse me sergeant?" the confused and slightly embarrassed Jansen asked.

"Listen private, I don't have a lot of time to waste. There are a lot of other soldiers I have to see after you. So, stop wasting my time and drop your pants. You're here because you think you have the clap, right?"

"Um, no. I picked up some shrapnel in my hand a couple of days ago. My captain noticed it and wanted me to come here and get it checked out. He was actually pretty pissed off that I hadn't come here earlier."

The medic's tone changed a little, "Oh, I just assumed that you were like all the other Joes that I've seen today. Typical grunts! Give them a couple of free hours and they go out and screw anything that has a pulse. Then they come in here by the droves begging for a cure, so they can take a leak without feeling like their dick is going to fall off. Okay, thanks for being an exception rather than the rule. What do you want me to look at?" the medic asked.

Jansen held out his hand that still had the field dressing on it. "I don't think it is anything serious, sergeant just got hit by a little shrapnel a couple of days ago. Nothing was embedded. I was just cut up a little."

The medic removed the field dressing, "It's best if you let me be the judge of that private." The medic spent the next few moments examining Jansen's hand. "It looks like you have been keeping the wounds pretty clean, but it is always better to come in, oftentimes what you think are minor wounds end up being more serious than you think. Can you wiggle your fingers for me?"

Jansen moved his fingers, they were a little sore, but other than that he did not have any trouble doing what he was told.

"Based on what I see, I don't think that there is going to be any permanent damage. Some of the cuts are quite long and kind of deep so I am going to give you a couple of sutures. Which means you are going to have to come back in about a week to have them removed. To save time, are you okay if I stitch you up without anesthesia?" asked the medic, "I still have a bunch of GIs to see before I can take a break."

Jansen agreed. The medic cleaned and sanitized the wounds, stitched up the longest cuts, gave Jansen an antibiotic shot, and sent him on his way. The speed and efficiency in which the sergeant worked on his hand told Jansen that this guy was not a Replacement. He had probably been in-country since Normandy and probably had plenty of practice doing this kind of thing in the field. Jansen had seen some green medics in combat puke or worse freeze up and just sit there doing nothing while an injured soldier was bleeding out in front of them.

This sergeant was different, even though Jansen's wounds were not serious, Jansen could see the sergeant putting his head down and performing the task ahead of him with a detached efficiency that comes from being a veteran of combat. It was a lesson that combat veterans had to learn if they were going to come out of the war with the ability to return to normal life back in the States.

After the medic finished stitching up his hand, Jansen stepped out of the tent into the cold dim light of the morning. It had been a short ride by truck in the morning to get from his unit to here, but now Jansen had to decide if he wanted to wait for a ride back to his unit, or if he wanted to walk back. If he walked, he would get back to his unit earlier than if he waited for the next truck.

If Jansen had known what the next few days would have in store for him, he might have decided on the easier of the two options. But, since he could not see into the future, he decided to spend half an hour or so walking the two miles back to his unit's staging area.

Jansen picked up his M1 carbine rifle and weaved his way through the other GIs waiting to see the medics and made his way toward the road that would take him back to his unit. As he approached the road Jansen saw an MP and asked if it was safe to walk back to his unit alone.

"There is plenty of traffic on this road, and we haven't had any reports of Krauts in the area, so you should be okay. But just to be safe, I would see if you could hitch a ride if you see that the traffic on the roads is beginning to die down."

With that Jansen made his way to the road that seemed to have a steady stream of military vehicles traveling on it.

The Kalenborn countryside was relatively flat and it felt good to be moving after standing around waiting to be seen by the medic for most of the morning. That is one of the things Jansen had learned as a soldier, standing around and waiting was oftentimes worse than marching or even being in combat. Waiting was an unavoidable part of being in the Army, but it could be downright miserable when the weather was bad.

Jansen began walking on the shoulder of the road that would take him back to his unit. He could feel his circulation returning to his legs and hands and for this first time in hours, he began to feel warmth returning to his body. Jansen was tall with dark hair and had a slim muscular body from the years spent working on his father's farm in South Dakota. Up until now the physical aspect of serving in the Army had been the easy part for Jansen. He felt that he had worked harder in the summers on the farm when they were harvesting corn and hay for the following year. Growing up on a farm during the Depression seemed more physically demanding than anything the Army had forced him to do so far.

As he walked by a small farm, he thought of his home and wondered how long it would be before he would be able to return to his family. He did not want to be here, he had been drafted after all, but he did have a sense of duty and felt that he had been called to do something honorable for his country. Having lived through the Great Depression, the idea of sacrificing for others and even his nation was not a foreign concept to him. Even though his life up until this point had not been easy, he knew others who were even less fortunate than him and had suffered much more hardship during the Depression than he and his family had.

There was a quiet confidence in him. Jansen was not cocky or arrogant, but he was someone who knew he had been through hard times and hard experiences and had come out the other side relatively unscathed. This had shown him that there are a lot of things in life that seem too hard, or even impossible to deal with at the time, that the average man can do if they can just focus on the task at hand.

Jansen caught the attention of a young German woman who was going outside to do her morning chores. She looked both innocent and jaded at the same time. It was as if this young woman had been forced to see and experience more in her short time on Earth than she should have at her age. Looking at her face Jansen could see both sadness and hope at the same time. He wondered how much of what he was seeing in her face was real, and how much of what he was

17

seeing was just his mind seeing what it wanted to see.

Jansen thought about shouting a greeting to her in German and then thought better of it, thinking of the long line of men at the aid tent waiting to be cured of infections they picked up from the local women. For all he knew, this young woman could have been one of the women responsible for giving the clap to one of GIs outside the medic tent he had just left.

Jansen quickly decided that since he was effectively alone, except for the steady stream of Army trucks and jeeps that were passing him on the road, that he should make it a priority to get back to his unit as quickly as possible.

The gloomy grayness of the landscape could only partially conceal the natural beauty of this area. One could imagine how the low rolling hills of this area would look in springtime, lit by a sun hung high in a deep blue cloudless sky, with every piece of vegetation a deep and healthy green.

But today, that was not the scene that Jansen saw as he walked back to his unit. He saw a dark gray world that had been ravaged by a war that had raged on for years at this point. A world that was marked in every direction with the signs of conflict; military vehicles that moved about, impact craters that dotted the landscape, and the ever-present occupation of soldiers, either German soldiers only a few weeks ago, or American soldiers today.

Jansen continued on his march back to his unit. He was a little more than halfway to where his unit was located when he noticed a change in the amount of traffic he was seeing on the road. Remembering the advice of the MP, he started trying to flag down a truck. It was not long before he was able to hitch a ride in the back of a deuce-and-a-half that was heading back to the general area of his unit. He was forced to ride in the back of the truck with the supplies. Jansen was alone with his thoughts and the various crates of military equipment it was hauling.

Jansen took out the little Bible that Chaplain Martin had given him. He opened it, there was a printed letter from President

Roosevelt talking about the importance of reading "the Sacred Book," and how the Bible has been a source of strength to people of many backgrounds.

Jansen quickly noted that this was not technically a Bible, it was just the New Testament. But it was small and something that he could always carry with him. He was thankful for the gift, and more so, thankful for his time with Chaplain Martin.

Before long he would be back with his unit, unaware of the events that were currently unfolding, and how over, the next few days, those events would impact him, his unit, and the course of the war.

CHAPTER TWO

MIKE COMPANY

March 7, 1945
1015 Hours

Jansen could hear the brakes screeching as the truck came to a stop. He looked out the back to see if he could see where they were. From what he could tell, the truck was close to where his company had been earlier that morning. He was thinking about jumping over the tailgate of the truck when one of the men from the cab came around to the back of the truck and dropped the tailgate for him to let him out.

"There you go buddy; your unit should be around here somewhere. And there's a bonus, the Red Cross donut truck is just over there, if you hurry you can catch it before it leaves."

Jansen thanked him, grabbed his rifle, and began quickly walking over to the Red Cross truck. There was a group of GIs standing around the truck drinking coffee out of canteen cups. The line was short, and Jansen took his place in the queue. He could smell the aroma of the coffee as the steam rose up into the cold morning air from the cups of the soldiers near him. Each man was enjoying the experience of having a hot drink to warm them up on a cold morning in March.

"Here you go soldier," came the voice of the Red Cross volunteer as she filled the canteen cup of the man in front of Jansen and handed him a donut.

"Thank you, ma'am," the soldier replied.

Jansen took his canteen out of its carrier and removed its canteen cup. When he came to the opening on the side of the truck a young woman wearing an American Red Cross uniform looked down at him from inside the truck. She seemed friendly and was probably not much older than Jansen himself. The volunteer had a warm smile and a pleasant demeanor.

"Coffee and donut soldier?" she asked.

"Yes ma'am," Jansen said as the Red Cross worker handed him a donut and filled his canteen cup with coffee. Jansen thanked her and began looking for a place to enjoy a short break before returning to his unit.

Jansen found a dry place to sit, drink his coffee, and eat his donut. Black coffee and a cake donut seemed like a real treat. Especially considering that he was in the European Theater of Operations. Back home people could still remember the deprivation that almost everyone faced during the Great Depression and now the United States was operating on a wartime economy where just about everything was rationed. In a weird way, Jansen considered himself to be lucky to have this simple treat.

Jansen took a bite of his donut and washed it down with some coffee. His hike back from the Battalion Aid tent had warmed him up, but after sitting in the back of a truck, much of the cold from that March morning had begun to seep back into his body. The coffee helped to warm him up and lifted his spirits.

It was surprising how a little thing like a few moments to enjoy a hot drink and a donut could affect Jensen's mood, but he definitely felt better and appreciated a break from the day to day rigors of life in an infantry unit fighting on the front lines in Germany in 1945. Maybe he was still remembering the kindness of Chaplain Martin and the lingering effects of that conversation. But, whatever the reason, right here, and right now, Jansen was feeling better than he had in quite some time.

Jansen took the last bite of his donut and continued to drink his coffee which was quickly cooling down in the cold morning air. He took a quick last swig and coffee and returned the canteen cup to its carrier.

Jansen got up, grabbed his M1 carbine, and headed over to the area where his company was located. Jansen looked out at what seemed to be a sea of chaos. The men of his regiment were housed in a collection of tents, shelter halves, and local farm buildings. It was not hard finding the group of tents where his unit was located.

Jansen had spent a fair amount of time sleeping on the ground in a shelter half since he had arrived in Germany. A shelter half is basically a pup tent that you share with another soldier. It is called a shelter half because each man is given half of the tent to carry and when it is time to set up the tent two soldiers connect their shelter halves together to form one small tent big enough for two men.

But tonight, Jansen did not need to worry about all that. His company had commandeered a farm building for the men to sleep in. It was not as nice as where the officers and support staff were sleeping, but it was better than sleeping on the cold ground in early March.

Jansen was assigned to Mike Company, Third Battalion, of the 311th Infantry Regiment. Mike Company had been in the ETO since December of 1944. So even though the veterans of the 311th had only been in combat for a few months, but they had seen enough combat in that time to gain valuable experience that the Replacements simply did not have. Jansen had proved himself to be a good soldier so far, but he had not lasted long enough to shake the label of "Replacement."

Jansen walked through the area. The terrain in this part of Germany was mostly flat farmland with gently rolling hills as you moved further away from the town of Kalenborn. Most of the farm buildings in the area were spaced a considerable distance apart. The buildings were made of weathered wood, but some of the older buildings were a mixture of wood and masonry construction.

Jansen, having grown up in America was not used to seeing buildings that had been around for hundreds of years, much less masonry farm buildings that could easily have been around since before Americans first settled in the area that would become his home state of South Dakota. Jansen wondered and marveled at the craftsmanship that allowed a structure as simple as a barn to survive for such a long time.

Jansen walked into a wooden farm building. As soon as he entered, he saw Harrison, his fellow machine gunner from his squad. Harrison was sitting on a crate that was pushed back against one of the walls of the barn. He was leaning up against the building and had one knee up and was writing something, probably a letter home.

Harrison was a skinny kid who spoke with a soft southern drawl. Even though Jansen and Harrison were about the same age and the same rank, that fact meant nothing in the dynamics of the unspoken hierarchy of a combat unit in 1945. Jansen was a Replacement and Harrison was a Veteran and that was the only thing that mattered.

Harrison looked up from what he was doing and saw Jansen approaching, "I hope you enjoyed your time off," he said somewhat sarcastically, "you'd better check in with Sergeant Collins and let him know you're back."

"Thanks, Harrison, have you seen him recently?"

"I think I heard the sarge yelling at someone a few minutes ago," Harrison motioned to one of the doors that led outside and then turned his attention back to what he was writing.

Jansen walked through the barn and walked back out into the cold March air hoping to find his Platoon Sergeant nearby. As Harrison had predicted, Sergeant Collins was just outside the barn looking extremely pissed off. Collins was a large man, and fit the role of a grizzled Platoon Sergeant to a tee, with broad shoulders and a barrel chest, he was a man who had chosen a life in the Army and seemed perpetually irritated by that decision. His face was flushed in the cool morning air. Who or what had made him mad was no longer in sight. Collins was walking toward the barn when he saw Jansen approaching.

Jansen tentatively approached Collins, "Good morning Sergeant, I'm back from sick-call."

"What's so good about it?" replied Collins as he looked at Jansen hoping to find some reason to lay into the young Replacement. But since he saw nothing obvious to complain about, Collins just flatly replied, "I'll let the Old Man know you made it back when I see him."

Jansen, feeling as though he had just dodged a bullet, looked at his watch. I t was getting close to noon, which meant that the cooks would be serving chow soon. Jansen had spent the last few days eating mostly K-rations and was looking forward to a hot meal. Serving in a forward combat unit meant that everything was constantly moving, even the support staff. The only way to find the chow line was to either stumble across it or ask around.

Jansen began looking for someone he could ask. Several soldiers were milling about the area occupied by Mike Company, but asking a Veteran, sergeant, or officer carried with it certain risks. As Jansen looked for someone to ask, he saw Ellison walking toward him with his M1 Garand slung over his shoulder. Ellison was also a Replacement, and the only person Jansen had gotten to know in his short time with his company.

When Jansen and Ellison arrived in the ETO, they were both assigned to the same squad, which was both a blessing and a curse. Since the Veterans did not talk much with the Replacements, having another Replacement in your squad meant that Jansen had someone to talk to. But since Replacements were usually only assigned where they were needed, it was rare that two replacements would be assigned to the same squad. That meant that Jansen and Ellison's squad had been hit harder than most, so the Veterans in their squad were even more reluctant to get to know, or even talk to, the Replacements.

Jansen walked over and greeted Ellison, "Hey Ellison, how are you doing?"

"Better than some, worse than most," came the reply, "Are you back from sick-call already?"

"Yeah, I walked most of the way back but was able to hitch a ride for some of it. Do you know where they are going to serve chow?" said Jansen as the two soldiers had now stopped walking and stood chatting near one of the farm buildings.

"Yeah, I think they set up on the other side of this building, I'm sure we will be able to see the line pretty soon, are you hungry?" Ellison asked.

"I'm not looking for the chow line because I'm full," came the snarky reply. Jansen had a dry sarcastic sense of humor and it only came out in conversations with people he knew and liked. These days Ellison was the only target for Jansen's barbs. Both men knew each other and were not offended by the occasional good-natured ribbing.

"Great, I guess that the line will form somewhere behind this building. I figure that guys have already started to line up. Let's go check it out," Ellison said as he began making his way around the building in question.

Ellison, like Jansen, had grown up on a farm, but his family moved from Kansas to California during the Depression after his father had lost their family farm in Kansas. Even though Ellison grew up in the Great Plains, he seemed more like the typical Californian. In many ways, he was the opposite of Jansen, open, easy to talk to, with blond hair, and an easy-going and laid back nature.

Jansen would have been drawn to Timothy Ellison even if their circumstances had not thrust them together. Ellison was just a nice kid who was always looking out for others. His appearance was average in almost every way. He was not particularly tall or muscular, his blond hair gave him an air of innocence. But Tim was the kind of person who was so good-natured and outgoing, that he would be the one person you would remember if you met him at a party.

Jansen and Ellison began walking toward the building hoping to find the chow line soon.

"If we don't see a line forming soon, we are going to have to wait, even if the cooks are almost ready to serve us," said Ellison, "Do you remember how much flack we took from the Veterans that one time for getting in line too early?"

Jansen recalled that experience well. It was shortly after they had joined the unit, the two of them saw that the cooks were getting ready to serve dinner and promptly got in line. One of the Veterans saw them at the beginning of the line and told them that they hadn't earned the right to just waltz up to the front of the line ahead of the men who had actually seen real combat.

When Jansen and Ellison rounded the edge of the farm building, they could see that the line had already begun to form. Jansen was especially glad because he was getting hungry. The cold of the morning combined with the walk he had taken to get back to his unit, meant that Jansen's body was telling him it was time to eat. He could feel his stomach growling under his uniform.

"The line looks pretty short, let's take our time and let some of the Veterans line up first," Ellison said while sizing up the growing line. Ellison would have let others in front of him even if he were not trying to avoid conflict with the Veterans. That was just the kind of guy he was.

Once the line had built up a little, Jansen and Ellison took their places in the queue. "Is there any news from back home worth mentioning?" Jansen asked.

"No not really, my dad still doesn't have enough money to buy a farm of his own, so he is still working on the same dairy farm. I told you about that place. That was the farm where my dad and I worked together before I was drafted."

Jansen liked hearing Ellison talk about his family. It was a way for Jansen to remember times with his own family in South Dakota. It took his mind off the day-to-day realities of being in a forward-deployed combat unit.

"What do you think you'll do when you finally go back home to

California?" Jansen asked.

"My dad has been trying to save up enough money so that he can buy a small farm somewhere, so I figured that I would take my mustering out pay and use that money to help him with that. I know how hard it was for him to see his farm in Kansas literally blowing away in the wind during the Dust Bowl. Losing his farm in Kansas was one of the worst things that ever happened to my dad. The way I figure it, if I can save enough money while I'm are over here, I think that he can buy a farm if we put our money together. I am quite sure that my dad will be able to pay me back eventually. But even if he can't, I will still have the GI Bill, so I will be able to go to college and get a good-paying job. Either way, I'll be fine. I just don't like the idea of my dad having to work for someone else for the rest of his life."

And that was why Jansen liked his friend from California. He was genuinely a good person. And he was not afraid to make sacrifices for others. And it seemed that Ellison did not just help others out of a sense of duty, but it seems to Jansen that Ellison enjoyed helping others, even if it was at his own expense.

Slowly some other soldiers from their company filed into line behind the two farm boys turned soldiers. Jansen and Ellison stopped talking to try to avoid drawing attention to themselves.

There was not anything particularly notable about the conversations that were going on around the two Replacements, except that they seemed to be almost expressly designed to exclude any input from the two green privates. But this was normal, Jansen and Ellison knew the drill. It was easier for Jansen, the more reserved of the two, to adjust to this treatment from the more seasoned soldiers, but it was much harder on the more outgoing Ellison.

While the two were waiting in the chow line and being ignored by just about everyone around them, Jansen looked up and saw Sergeant Parker approaching the chow line. Parker was Jansen's squad leader and immediately recognized Jansen and Ellison and proceeded to walk up to the two Replacements.

Parker was Regular Army, meaning he had decided to make a career of the Army before the war. Jansen's body stiffened a little as Parker approached. Parker walked straight up to Jansen and Ellison and looked them in the eyes. Now Jansen could see the ubiquitous fleas in Parker's eyebrows. Personal hygiene simply was not a thing for this man who had spent his entire adult life in the Army.

"You two won't mind if I cut in front of you, now will you?" Parker asked in a thick New York accent.

Ellison replied, "Not at all, help yourself, sergeant."

Parker was much like any other Veteran in how he treated the Replacements, but for some reason, he would go out of his way to show that as a Veteran and a sergeant he was their superior in just about every way that currently mattered. Jansen thought that this was comical because even though Jansen came from very humble beginnings, he looked down on Parker. Jansen simply saw Parker as a man who was unclean and so uncouth and not worthy of his respect.

Parker began quietly chatting with the men in front of him in line. Jansen and Ellison kept their distance from the crass New York sergeant because they did not want to hear what he was saying, and they definitely did not want one of those fleas to jump off Parker's body and jump onto them. Life in combat is hard enough. There was no reason to make it worse by picking up fleas, or worse yet, lice by stupidly being too close to a man that was known to have both.

The chow line moved in a quick, orderly fashion, and soon Jansen and Ellison were looking for a place to sit and enjoy their food. The two found a tree nearby. The two soldiers sat down to eat their meal. Jansen's body relaxed as he stretched out his legs. He had been walking or standing almost the entire morning. It felt good to finally take a load off his tired legs.

Jansen began to eat his food in silence. He knew that this would drive the chatty Ellison nuts, but he was cold, tired, and hungry. Conversation could wait, his body was telling him that right now there were more important things than idle chatter. And it was always better to eat chow in the field while it was still hot, that was why they did not waste any time looking for a place to eat inside one of the farm buildings. Any available space inside would most likely be already taken, and even if they were lucky enough to find someplace indoors to enjoy their meal, there was no guarantee that a Veteran wouldn't come along and demand that they give up their spot anyway.

After eating about half of his food, Jansen's stomach had stomped rumbling and he decided to take a less hurried approach to eating his lunch, thus, allowing time for conversation between bites. He was fairly sure that the silence between himself and Ellison since entering the chow line was driving his friend crazy.

"I talked to a chaplain today when I went to sick-call," Jansen finally said as he continued to eat.

"Really, what was that like?"

Jansen did not want to talk, but he realized his mistake by starting the conversation. And with a subject that would pretty much force him to carry the discussion. Jansen decided to keep it simple in hopes that Ellison would take over.

"He seemed like a good guy, he gave me a pocket New Testament," Jansen pulled out the pocket "Bible" that Chaplain Martin had given him earlier. Jansen could not bring himself to call it a Bible, that was his pedantic nature taking over, that and his deep respect for Scripture.

Ellison respectfully leafed through the book not looking at anything in particular and handed it back to Jansen.

"That will be nice for you to have when we are in the field. How was your trip to sick-call anyway?" Ellison asked, changing the subject.

"Nothing major happened, I just got a few stitches. At first, they thought I was there because I had VD," Jansen laughed, "I guess they'd never met a strait-laced farm boy from South Dakota before."

"Yeah, Jansen, but honestly it wouldn't kill you to let yourself have fun every once in a while. What's the matter, do you have a girl back home or something?"

"No, it's nothing like that," Jansen replied. The truth was that Jansen never had to worry about women or girls. His education ended in the 8th grade in a small one-room schoolhouse. He never went to high school, and even if he had, it would not have been a place to meet girls, given how small his hometown was.

This may have been for the better because Jansen's reserved nature would not have gotten him noticed in a regular high school anyway. "I never even had the chance to go to a big high school, and even if I had, I wouldn't have had any money to take a girl out on a date," Jansen said.

"It's not like I am a huge expert on the subject either, but I have been known to go on a date or two in my time, and I have to say, there is nothing quite like spending time with a beautiful girl," Ellison answered. Knowing Ellison as he did, Jansen had no trouble believing that he was probably a hit with the ladies back home.

"I'll have to take your word for it," Jansen said as he was finishing up his meal, "If I ever do get lucky enough to find the right girl, I'll make sure that you'll be the first to know. But I think that I should go check in with Harrison. I am sure there is something that he wants me to do for him."

With that, Jansen shoveled that last few bites of food into his mouth and waited for Ellison to do the same.

"Yeah," Ellison replied, "while you were gone, I saw him sitting around all morning. I am sure there is something that needs to be done that he is waiting for you to do."

The two young men got up and walked back over to where the cooks were serving lunch and put their dirty trays in an ever-growing pile.

Jansen and Ellison said goodbye to each other and went their separate ways. Jansen made his way back to the barn where he had last seen Harrison. Harrison was still sitting in the same place, but now instead of writing, he was eating his lunch.

"Hey Harrison, I talked to Sergeant Collins and had lunch. Is there anything we are supposed to do?" Jansen asked, knowing full well that there was probably some job Harrison was putting off until he could get Jansen to do it for him.

"Yeah, we haven't fully dismantled and cleaned M1919 in a while, Sergeant Collins wants that done as soon as possible, so you should probably start working on that," Harrison said between bites of food. The M1919 Harrison mentioned was an M1919A6 Browning machine gun that Harrison and Jansen operated together.

Jansen knew that this was about as much conversation he could expect from Harrison. In many ways, Harrison was a typical Veteran. But because they had to work together as part of a two-man machine gun team, that meant that Jansen was treated better by Harrison than he was by the other Veterans who basically just ignored him. That being said, Jansen knew that Harrison probably had plenty of time to field strip and clean the maching gun himself after Sergeant Collins told him it needed to be done, but waiting for Jansen to return and then forcing his fellow machine gunner to do the work was just one more way of reminding Jansen that Harrison was a Veteran and Jansen was a lowly Replacement.

Jansen did not argue and got to work on the machine gun. Stripping and cleaning the M1919 could be a quick job or it could take quite a while. But with the cold wet weather they had been through in the last few days, Jansen knew it was neither going to be a quick nor an easy job. Especially since he knew he would be doing all the work himself and, most likely, would not be helped at all by his fellow machine gunner.

Jansen spent a good chunk of the afternoon disassembling and cleaning the machine gun. In a way, he did not mind the work. It gave him something to do, and even though he was still learning his role in this unit, learning the mechanical nature of things was something that came easily to him. In the short time he had been a machine gunner, he had mastered the art of field stripping and cleaning the M1919. And the way Jansen looked at it, if he did the work himself, at least he knew that the job would be done right, reducing the chance of the gun jamming when they needed it to work in combat.

After his job was done, Jansen decided that he had earned some time to himself. He found a place in the barn to sit down, pulled out the New Testament the chaplain had given him, and started thumbing through it. His mind went back to earlier that morning when he had talked to Chaplain Martin. A slight grin came across his face as he remembered that conversation.

Jansen was not reading any specific passage in the Bible when he saw Sergeant Parker approaching out of the corner of his eye. Jansen quickly closed the small book and slipped it into his pocket.

"Hey Jansen, what are you reading?"

Jansen rose to his feet to address his superior, "Nothing sergeant, just flipping through a pocket Bible the chaplain gave me this morning," Jansen couldn't believe that he called it a "Bible," but he wanted to get out of this conversation as quickly as possible and he knew if he called it a New Testament, it would require an additional amount of explanation that would only prolong this unwanted discussion with Sergeant Parker.

"Jansen, if I ever catch you reading that thing when we are in combat and we have something real to worry about, I'll throw that damn thing away and then I'll beat some sense into you. Do you understand, private?"

Before joining the Army, Parker had worked on the docks of New York during the depression to help out his family. Working on the docks and unloading heavy crates and sacks had given him a broad, muscular physique. The physical activity of being in a light infantryman had not changed Parker's large imposing frame. And Parker had earned a reputation of being a bit of a brawler, so Jansen did not doubt that Parker would eventually follow through on his threat.

"No problem sergeant, is there anything else?" Jansen replied.

"Back home you can waste time with that kind of nonsense, but here in combat, you need to keep your head in the game, or it is going to get shot off. Keep your head down and maybe the CO won't have to write a letter home to your parents telling them that their son did something stupid in combat and was killed because he was reading some dumb book?"

"Yes, sergeant."

"As you were," Parker said as he began to turn and walk away.

Jansen was a little shaken, the Veterans did not usually engage the Replacements like that, and he was not used to being threatened. Jansen came from such a small town that he had never even been in a real fight. And now he was halfway across the world fighting and killing Nazi soldiers in combat. Jansen took a deep breath and decided to see if the cooks had started serving dinner. He was hoping to be able to turn in a little early and put this day behind him.

Jansen just was not the type of person who could let an experience like that happen without thinking it over, or maybe even overthinking it. He already knew that Parker did not like him, but what the sergeant had said seemed to Jansen to be more than Parker picking on the new guy. What was it that Parker said before he walked away, something about keeping your head down or being killed in combat?

Jansen wondered if this was Parker's brash New Yorker's way of telling him that he did not want to see another Replacement die in combat needlessly. Maybe, Parker, in his own way, was trying to look out for Jansen. But then again, Jansen told himself that he may just be overthinking things.

Jansen sat down and lit a cigarette, reflecting on the day's events, and his recent dust-up with Parker. It was nice to have a break from fighting, getting a few hot meals, and an easy day of duties in a rear area. Jansen finished his cigarette and looked at his watch. Most likely the chow line would be forming soon, so he began to walk back to the area where he had been served lunch.

Soon he found the chow line, it was long enough that he figured he could slide into line without pissing anyone off. He was thinking of his life back in the states and wondering what it would be like going home after the war. He wondered how his family was doing, or even what they were doing.

His thoughts came back to the present when he heard two soldiers in line in front of him talking. He tried to keep to himself and never wanted to be caught eavesdropping, but he could make out them talking about a battle in a nearby town that was on the Rhine River and some vague talk about a bridge, but that was about as much as he could glean from the conversation before the two men changed the subject.

Jansen got his food and sat down with a group of replacements from other platoons and quietly ate his chow. After dinner, he did a little reading and then went to bed. It was a little after 2000 hours when he finally fell asleep. Considering how hard some of his days in-country had been so far, this day was not that bad. He was tired enough that he fell asleep quickly. Jansen did not realize that the short bit of conversation he overheard while in the chow line about a town on the edge of the Rhine would very soon consume the attention of the world. And that he would find himself right in the middle of an amazing turn of events that would have a huge impact on the war against the Nazis.

CHAPTER THREE

ZERO THREE THIRTY HOURS

March 8, 1945
0330 Hours

Jansen was high crawling on his elbows and dragging his body through the dirt as bullets whizzed over his head. There were men all around him working at getting through this area as quickly as possible while staying as low to the ground as they could to protect themselves from the constant stream of bullets that were flying only inches above their heads. Keeping your head down was an important skill to learn for any infantryman.

Just then Jansen heard someone scream, "Snake!"

He glanced over and saw a fellow soldier face to face with a venomous snake. To his horror, the soldier jumped to his feet. Jansen watched as one bullet tore through the man's abdomen and a second hit him in the chest. The whole scene seemed to play out before Jansen in slow motion. The wounded soldier's body went limp and he began to fall to the ground. The snake slithered away, no longer posing any threat if he ever had in the first place. The blood from the bullet holes began to seep into the man's uniform.

Jansen yelled, "Cease fire! Man down!" And crawled over to the bleeding soldier as the rifle fire was suddenly silenced. Now that he was closer Jansen could see how serious the wounds were. The man's face had lost all its color and now had an ashen appearance. He could also see that the soldier was losing blood quickly.

Jansen grabbed the man's shoulder and rolled him over on his back. Just doing that simple act was unnerving for Jansen. The man's wounds were so large that just by rolling the man over, Jansen had accidentally touched the edge of one of the exit wounds. The soldier was now laying on his back. Jansen looked down at his hands and could see that they were covered in blood.

The dying soldier looked into Jansen's eyes and said, "I'm not going to die, am I, Jansen?"

Jansen had no response and just looked at the dying man's face. This was the closest Jansen had been to someone who was dying, and he honestly did not know what to do.

The soldier suddenly began calling his name, "Jansen! Jansen!"

Jansen opened his eyes, Ellison was shaking him, "Jansen, Jansen, you need to get up!"

For a moment Jansen was in the foggy state in between sleep and consciousness. As his mind began to clear, he realized that it was Ellison who was talking to him, not the man from his dream. What Jansen had been dreaming about was not some random nightmare, it was something that Jansen had experienced when he was in basic training. The real-life soldier in Jansen's dream had been shot during a live-fire exercise and had died from his wounds.

That is something that most people do not know or think about, that death in the military is not limited to those who die on the battlefield. Plenty of people die in training as well. But for those who have experienced both, death is just as real whether it happens in combat or not.

Jansen was awake now and looked at Ellison, "What the hell is going on?"

"Sergeant Collins is telling us to grab our gear, lock up all our personal items, then form up outside and await orders. They're sending us back to the front."

Jansen and his unit had bedded down the night before in the farm building his unit had commandeered the previous day. Jansen wanted to go to sleep a little earlier than the rest of the men in his unit, so he found a quiet corner of the building to sleep the night before.

Jansen got out of his bedroll and began getting dressed. For many soldiers, the time between when you get up on a cold morning, and when you are fully dressed and have started to warm up in your uniform is always unpleasant. And this cold morning in March was no exception. Jansen felt like the cold morning air was penetrating straight through his body as he got dressed as quickly as possible. He was still a little tired from the march back from sick-call the day before. He was hoping for a good night's sleep for a change. He had not planned on getting up so early.

"What time is it?" Jansen asked, still coming out of the fog of being asleep as he pulled on his boots.

"Zero-three-thirty hours. I've gotta go and get the rest of my gear ready," came the reply as Ellison walked over to where he had been sleeping and began packing up his gear.

Jansen began to envy his friend. Ellison was on a regular fire team and carried an M1 Garand which weighed ten pounds. But since Jansen was on a machine gun crew, he carried an M1 Carbine which weighed only five pounds. The problem was that, between Jansen and Harrison they also had to carry the M1919A6 Browning machine gun which weighed 31 pounds, as well as all the ammo for the machine gun. All this added up to a lot of extra weight that Jansen had to carry when their unit went into combat. The extra weight was in addition to everything else the average infantryman had to carry.

Jansen finished getting dressed, gathering up, and donning his combat gear. He then headed over to talk to Harrison. He knew the drill; they would have to check the Browning and ensure that it was working properly. Then they would need to go to supply and get the ammo for the machine gun and transfer the belts of ammo from the ammo cans into satchels so that the ammunition would be easier to carry.

Jansen and Harrison got everything together quickly and headed outside to where the company was forming up. Harrison grabbed the satchels with the ammo belts and headed outside. Harrison usually did not talk to Jansen much and often just assumed that Jansen would grab the Browning machine gun. That was how it had been ever since Jansen joined the unit a couple of weeks ago. Harrison would just assume that Jansen would be carrying the awkward machine gun most of the time. But whenever they were in a firefight, Jansen was usually relegated to feeding the ammo belts into the machine gun while Harrison did most of the shooting.

This was another way for Harrison to remind Jensen that there was a difference between the Veterans and the Replacements. There was a hierarchy, a pecking order, and Harrison's actions were a constant reminder to Jansen that he just was not that important in the eyes of his fellow machine gunner.

But to be honest, Jansen was not usually itching to fire the machine gun in combat anyway. Jansen was a good soldier, but he knew that the point of being on a machine gun crew was to injure or kill as many enemy combatants in the shortest amount of time as possible. Jansen was completely capable of carrying out any operation with skill and precision. But unlike many of the fellow infantrymen, Jansen considered the gravity of what he was doing more than most. The death and destruction he was personally causing to fellow human beings whenever he fought in combat did not go unnoticed by the young soldier.

Jansen grabbed the thirty-one-pound machine gun, threw it over his shoulder, and walked outside to where his company was forming up. Standing around in formation was a thing that Jansen just assumed would be something that only happened while he was in basic training. And he was genuinely surprised that it was one of the first things that happened when he arrived in-country and was assigned to Mike Company. But, like many things in the Army, some things seem like silly traditions that end up having a real-life application. The formation was a great way to account for every man in your unit in a short amount of time. Especially in a situation like this, when the unit was coming off a day of rest and recuperation and was being ordered to head out in the middle of the night. Commanders needed to know where everyone was in a short amount of time. And the military formation was the quickest way to get that information.

Jansen had his M1 Carbine slung across his back and was holding the M1919 along the side of his body, the butt of the machine gun was at his feet and the tip of the barrel reached up to his shoulder. It was a beast of a weapon and there was absolutely no way to carry it comfortably while marching. Jansen was not looking forward to carrying it and was hoping that, maybe, they would be riding in trucks to wherever they were headed.

The men of Mike Company formed ranks to ensure that everyone was present. The Company Commander walked over and called the men to attention. It was still the middle of the night; it was about three hours before the sun would begin to rise. There was not much moonlight seeping through the overcast sky, so Jansen really couldn't see Captain Horn very well as the CO stood in front of his men.

Horn addressed the men, "The 9th Armored Division has captured an intact bridge across the Rhine. Ike wants every available unit to converge on the bridgehead. We are awaiting orders. Support staff will work on packing up and the combat platoons will depart as soon as we know where we will be meeting up with the rest of the regiment. In the meantime, you men are dismissed. Just stay in the area and don't wander off without checking with your platoon sergeant first."

The men milled about in the cold night air, Jansen removed the bedroll from his web gear, dropped it on the ground, and used it as a cushion to sit on. Waiting is one of the hardest things you have to do as a soldier, especially when weather conditions are not ideal. Jansen was happy that it was not raining, being cold and tired was bad enough, but being cold, tired, and wet would have been worse. He lit a cigarette and tried not to fall asleep.

Ellison came over and sat down next to Jansen, "How are you doing?"

Jansen replied, "Tired, I think I shouldn't have decided to walk back from sick-call yesterday. I could have just waited for a ride."

"Hopefully, all this will be a whole lot of nothing. I wonder how long we are going to have to wait here. But that is the Army for you, hurry up and wait. Sometimes I think that command hands out medals to officers who can make their soldiers stand around and do nothing the longest amount of time," Ellison quipped.

Jansen was glad that his friend had come over, it would make waiting more bearable and would help him to stay awake, "I don't know about you, but I'd rather not be sitting out here in the cold all night, waiting to move out," Jansen replied.

"I wouldn't hold your breath; these things always seem to take a long time. You'd think after a hundred and seventy years the Army would have figured out a way to let us grunts rest while the generals figure out where everyone needs to go. Sometimes I think officers figure that if they have to be up trying to figure out what to do, that it only makes sense that we have to be awake too." As Ellison was speaking, Sergeant Collins came over. The two green soldiers jumped to their feet in the presence of their NCO.

"Jansen, the captain wants to talk to you," Collins said gruffly, it seemed that even the veteran platoon sergeant was mad that he was not still in bed.

"Yes sergeant," Jansen replied, "do you know why he wants to see me?"

"No idea private, he is over there. I wouldn't sweat it though; he didn't seem pissed off when he asked to see you."

Collins' response was not that comforting for Jansen. But he also was not overly worried. Jansen felt he had been successful at flying under the radar in his short time with his unit, so it was unlikely that he had done something that would warrant negative attention from his CO. He just hoped the captain was not going to deliver some bad news from back home.

Jansen could not figure out how he was supposed to report to Captain Horn while lugging a machine gun so he asked Ellison if he could watch it for a couple of minutes. Jansen walked over to where Horn was standing, came to attention, saluted, and said, "Private Jansen reports as ordered sir."

Horn returned the salute, "At ease, private. I just got a note from medical. They say that the wounds they treated you for today qualify you for a Purple Heart. I agree with them, but I thought I would ask you before submitting the paperwork. What do you think?"

"Sir, I don't think a couple of stitches is enough for a Purple Heart. I would rather you didn't put me in for it, if that's okay," Jansen replied, relieved that he was called over to see his CO for something so trivial and that wasn't something serious or important.

"Okay, I won't put you in for it. It'll save me some paperwork. Thank you, Jansen, that is all," replied Horn.

"Yes sir," Jansen replied.

"You are dismissed soldier," Captain Horn said to Jansen. Horn then walked over to his jeep and began chatting with his radio operator.

He had not gotten to know many of the Replacements yet and Jansen was no exception. But Captain Horn's opinion of Jansen was bolstered a little by their brief exchange. He admired the stoic humility of the young soldier as he walked over to a jeep.

Jansen walked back over to where he left Ellison with the machine gun. Ellison was sitting on his field pack, smoking a cigarette, "You owe me, Jansen. To protect the machine gun, I had to fight off two squads of Nazis with nothing but my E-tool while you were gone."

"Really!?! Collins should recommend you for a medal for your bravery," Jansen said dryly.

Ellison had a mind like that, his brain was constantly switching gears. His constant good-natured ribbing is one of the things that made him such a likable guy.

"So, what did the old man want to talk to you about?" Ellison asked.

Jansen paused, he didn't want to talk about his conversation with Horn, but he felt that he had to at least attempt some level of honesty with his friend, "He just wanted to talk to me about my visit to sick-call this morning."

"Why did Horn care about that?" Ellison asked in a confused tone. The reason for Ellison's confusion was because COs usually did not take a personal interest in such mundane matters concerning their men.

"Horn was the one who noticed the wounds on my hands and told me to go to sick-call in the first place," Jansen replied.

Just then, Sergeant Collins came by and gave the platoon permission to spread out as long as they stayed within earshot, "When I give the order for the platoon to form up, you bastards have only sixty seconds to be in formation," were his exact words. The men of the platoon all moved off in groups to find a more comfortable place to sit while they were waiting for their orders.

Jansen and Ellison found a crate to sit on near where their platoon had just formed up. The two soldiers began chatting in the cold early morning air. It was not freezing, but it was still cold, the temperature was probably in the mid-30s if they had to guess. And neither of the men wanted to have to sit on the cold ground waiting for orders.

"Man, it's cold," said Ellison, taking off his gloves and rubbing his hands together then quickly putting his gloves back on, "I have a question for you. Did you ever see the pictures of Roman soldiers in the history books?" Ellison asked.

Since Jansen never went to high school there were a lot of things he had not been exposed to, and ancient Roman history was one of those things. He had never gotten much beyond the basics of reading, writing, and math.

"No, I don't think I have," Jansen answered.

"Well, as I understand it, the Romans made it all the way up to England as their empire expanded, and the Roman soldiers in the books are dressed in little skirts and metal armor that left their arms exposed."

Given the situation, Jansen could see where his friend was going with this conversation, "Go on."

Ellison continued, "How in the hell did those guys survive the winter if that is all they were allowed to wear? They must have frozen their nuts off. Here I am with probably twice the clothing they had, and I can't even feel my toes."

"Yeah, I suppose you're right," Jansen replied.

"And that reminds me of another thing. Do you suppose that when the Romans soldiers were in formation and had to count off they would go, 'eye, eye eye, eye eye eye, eye vee, vee, vee eye,' you know, because they would be counting using Roman numerals?" Ellison said with a chuckle.

Jansen laughed. He had been taught Roman numerals, mostly because it was still common to see Roman numerals on old Grandfather clocks and pocket watches. So, this time he got the joke without needing any explanation.

He was glad to have someone like Ellison to pass the time with, he was still cold, but he welcomed anything that would help take his mind off being cold, tired, and bored.

Jansen and Ellison sat there chatting about nothing important for the next few hours. Occasionally one of them would take a short break to "rest his eyes" while the other stayed awake in case an NCO or officer happened to walk by. That way, whoever was awake could nudge the other to make sure that they did not get caught sleeping.

Just before sunrise Collins called the platoon over to the assembly area and gave the men K-rations. This meant two things to

43

the men. First, the commander did not think there was enough time for the kitchen to serve up a hot meal for breakfast. And second, it meant that Mike Company would probably be eating K-rations for the foreseeable future. Each man grabbed three K-rations, one for each of the day's meals. Jansen was not looking forward to eating stone-cold canned meat and beans for breakfast.

After sunrise was a particularly frustrating time to be in the field with nothing to do but wait. Even though the sky was overcast, it is natural to think that sunrise will bring some extra warmth. And for soldiers just sitting outside with nothing to do but wait, it can be frustrating when the light of the morning comes, but the warmth the sun should bring is still hours away.

Shortly after eight o'clock, Jansen heard their first sergeant bellow, "Company, fall in!"

CHAPTER FOUR

THE ATTACK

March 8, 1945
0730 Hours

Jansen and Ellison grabbed their gear and rushed over to the assembly area. Jansen carried the M1919 on his shoulder as he quickly took his place in the formation. Sergeant Collins did a fair amount of yelling, especially at the soldiers who were not making it into formation as quickly as he would like. With a few exceptions, the platoon was able to form up pretty close to the benchmark of sixty seconds he had set earlier.

Mike Company's First Sergeant walked to the front of the formation, came to attention, and yelled, "Company!"

The Platoon Sergeants echoed in unison, "Platoon!"

"Attention!" the first sergeant called out into the night as the entire company came to attention. Captain Horn walked over to the first sergeant, saluted his NCO, and then addressed the company, "Well boys, we are headed for Meckenheim to meet up with the rest of the regiment. From there we will be going to Remagen. We have arranged for trucks to take us from here to the German side of the Rhine. Squad leaders and platoon sergeants, make sure you have a good headcount, load up your men and get ready to move out. Dismissed!"

Sergeant Parker went over and talked to Sergeant Collins, then came back to his squad and started barking orders. Soon his squad had been directed to the truck they would be taking to Meckenheim. Once the men began getting into the truck, there was an animated discussion amongst the squad leaders about how many men they should load into the back of the deuce-and-a-half and whether or not they should try to keep the squads together on the trucks. Eventually, it was agreed not to split up the squads and that they would throw a few extra men on each truck so that the squad leaders could keep an eye on their men.

This meant that the Replacements would have to sit on the floor of the truck between the two rows of drop-down seats on the side of the truck bed. When Parker picked Jansen to be one of the "volunteers" who would be sitting on the bed of the truck, Jansen begged Harrison to take the M1919. Jansen did not want the newly cleaned and maintained weapon laying in a truck bed, possibly picking up some dirt that might cause a malfunction later. In this instance, Harrison did not mind making the switch, because since they were riding in trucks, having the machine gun was not that much of a burden.

So, at 0812 hours on the morning of March 8th, Mike Company loaded up into trucks and headed out to Meckenheim. The roads were already extremely busy. Every US Army unit in the area was trying to converge on Remagen and there were only so many roads that led there.

Once on the road, the trucks made slow progress. Jansen was sitting on the floorboards of the truck and could feel every bump that the truck hit as it lumbered along on the rural German road. Jansen was already tired and cold, and after riding on the floor of this truck, soon he was going to be sore as well.

Jansen still had not seen much combat and knowing that at the end of this infernal trip he would be thrust into combat was

46

something he didn't want to think about. But at the same time, he found himself repeatedly dwelling on that fact. He felt his gut tighten and his hands became jittery. He pulled out a pack of cigarettes and lit one, just to give himself something to do and hopefully take his mind off where he was and where he was going.

Ellison was sitting on the bed of the truck just in front of Jansen. But they knew better than to talk. For one thing, it would be impractical, and more importantly because it would probably draw the ire of the Veterans they were riding with.

Jansen looked up at the overcast sky. The truck he was riding in could have a canvas top installed on it to cover the men riding in the back. But when riding into combat soldiers generally preferred the ability to see potential dangers over the advantage of being protected from the elements. For this reason, the truck's canvas cover had been removed.

This part of their trip was well wooded, with trees growing right up to the side of the road they were traveling on. Jansen could not help but think that if the circumstances were different, this might be a nice place to visit. Even at this time of the year, as the landscape was coming out of its winter slumber and even though there was still was not much green vegetation, Jansen could appreciate the potential beauty of this area of Germany.

The trees were bare, the leaves that adorned their branches during summer and fall were now long gone. Growing up on the plains of South Dakota, Jensen had never really seen anything like a real forest. In fact, until he joined the Army, Jansen had never traveled more than 50 miles from his hometown. He had seen trees before, but he had never seen the dense forests like those of Germany that rolled over the landscape for miles in every direction.

The convoy was moving out of the wooded area of the German hills and into an area of open farmland. The trucks were well spaced out so that they would not present an easy target for an attack from the Germans. But the traffic on the road made it difficult for the drivers to keep as far away from the truck in front of them as they would like.

The convoy of trucks continued down the country roads as they slowly passed pastures and farmland with farmer's cottages and barns interspersed along the way. Now that the terrain was less wooded, the soldiers did not worry about the remote possibility of some small group of German soldiers hiding out in the trees somewhere waiting to attack the convoy. And now the likelihood of a small unit of Nazis hiding out in this open area was extremely unlikely.

When they had traveled about half of the six and a half miles from Kalenborn to Meckenheim the men of Jansen's squad heard the drone of aircraft engines.

"What's that?" yelled Harrison.

The men in the back of the deuce-and-a-half turned toward the noise to see if they could spot the incoming plane. Ellison and Jansen were facing backward and had a good view out of the back of the truck.

"I see them! They are right there," called out Ellison as he pointed at the two incoming German planes.

Jansen looked at where Ellison was pointing and spotted the two planes. Jansen, who had started his training as an anti-aircraft gunner before being switched over to the infantry, could remember enough of his previous training to know that the two planes were Ju 87 Stuka dive bombers. Most likely these planes were part of Germany's attempt to blow up the bridge the Americans had captured at Remagen.

These two pilots had probably just peeled off from their group after failing to bring down the bridge with their bombs. Jansen figured that the German pilots were just looking to inflict some damage on the American convoys converging on Remagen before heading back to base. With all the American anti-aircraft guns placed along the Rhine to protect the bridge from attacks by the Luftwaffe, the Stuka pilots probably decided that attacking a random convoy would be a safe bet.

The two planes dove out of the sky and lined up on the convoy preparing to strafe the trucks with their 7.62-millimeter forward-mounted guns. Those bullets would not be highly effective in destroying the trucks, but they could certainly inflict heavy damage to a group of soldiers packed tightly together in the back of those trucks.

"Everyone, get out and find cover!" yelled Parker as the truck came to a stop and the soldiers and the drivers of the truck jumped out of the vehicle.

There was not much cover, but luckily for the men traveling in the truck with Jansen, there was a farm building with a high stone foundation and a dry irrigation ditch that the men could put between themselves and the oncoming Stukas. Almost everyone in the truck had either found cover or was nearly safe when the dive bombers started firing.

Other trucks loaded with soldiers in the convoy were not as lucky. They were caught out in the open with no close options for cover.

After the first pass, the Stukas did not circle back around for a second pass, either because they were low on ammo, low on fuel, or just because they decided not to press their luck. Jansen's squad was spread out between the irrigation ditch and the barn. When the coast was clear Parker gathered his men.

"Is everyone okay? Did anyone get injured?" Parker asked.

The response from the squad was mixed with colorful language about the Nazi pilots that had attacked them and the possibility that they were born under less than honorable circumstances. Aside from that, nobody reported any injuries. They had all made it through the attack unscathed.

Sergeant Collins came over to check on the men.

"Parker, how are you doing?" Collins' voice was oddly calm given the situation.

"No injuries Collins, what do you want us to do?"

"Just hold tight for now Parker, I'll be back in a bit after I am done checking in with the other squads."

As Collins walked off to check on the other squads in his platoon, he noticed soldiers from another squad that had been hit.

"Parker, send some of your men over to help these men until the medics can get to them."

"Ellison and Jansen go over and see what you can do," Parker told the two Replacements.

"Of course, he would send us," Ellison complained, "the two guys with the least amount of experience with this sort of thing. I think he is secretly hoping that one of us will lose our lunch, then Parker and the other Veterans can have a good laugh at our expense."

"Hopefully, it won't be that bad," said Jansen and the two walked over to the wounded men.

One of the company medics, a young man from Ohio named Brian O'Connor, was already working on a man who had been hit in the gut and had already lost a lot of blood. When O'Connor saw Jansen and Ellison approaching, he turned to them and said, "go check on that private over there, he's been hit in the shoulder. I'll get over to help you as soon as I can."

Jansen and Ellison made it over to the wounded man. The medic did not need to tell either of them that his man had been hit in the shoulder. Blood was seeping into his uniform from the wound and the man's left arm was laying, limp, against his body.

Jansen and Ellison looked at each other and then quietly went to work. Ellison's chatty and outgoing nature would disappear in situations like this. It was almost like he knew when it was a good time to be cracking jokes, and when it was better to just be quiet. And Jansen being the quieter of the two would just put his head down and work at the task at hand without talking. In that respect they were both excellent soldiers, they both could focus on what needed to be done, do what they were told to do, and do it well.

Ellison rolled the man over on his uninjured side looking for the exit wound. The wounded soldier screamed as he was moved. There seemed to be almost nothing holding the man's arm in place. There was a grapefruit-sized crater in the man's shoulder just above his armpit. The man was bleeding, but there was not any spurting blood coming from the wound. Jansen prayed that this meant that the artery to the man's arm was still intact. This was not the first time Jansen had been sent to help the medics with men wounded in combat. Talking to the medics he had learned that if an artery were severed, there was only a small chance that the doctors would be able to save an injured limb. At least this guy had a chance to keep his arm.

Ellison tore away some of the man's uniform to expose the exit wound. He could see right into the man's shoulder. He tore open a packet of sulfa powder and sprinkled it into the open wound then he opened his field dressing packet and shoved it into the wound trying to use the bandage to fill up as much of the gaping hole as he could. The injured man screamed.

Jansen yelled at O'Connor, "Hey, doc, do you have anything we can give this guy for the pain? His shoulder looks really bad."

"Yeah, I'll be over in a sec. I can give you some morphine if you are okay injecting him yourself."

"Sure," Jansen replied. He had grown up on a dairy farm during the Depression and had learned how to give injections to livestock on his father's farm because their family could not afford to pay a vet every time one of their livestock was sick. Jansen figured that this should not be that different.

Jansen walked over to O'Connor who had his kit bag next to him.

"Here you go," O'Connor said as he handed Jansen a morphine syrette.

Jansen ran back to the wounded man, shoved the needle into the man's shoulder, and squeezed the back of the syrette pushing the morphine into the man's body.

After Ellison was done working on the exit wound, they rolled the injured man over onto his back and began looking for the entry wound on the other side of the man's shoulder. The injured man's body began to relax a little as the morphine was beginning to do its job. Jansen found the entry wound and used the field dressing and sulfa powder from his web gear to treat the wound. Just as they were wrapping up, the medic made it over to check on the wounded soldier Jansen and Ellison had worked on.

"Looks like you two did a pretty good job," O'Connor said approvingly. "I'll take it from here."

As O'Connor was working, he turned to Jansen, "It looks like you had to use your own field dressing and sulfa on this guy. There are extra field dressing packets and sulfa in my kit bag. Go ahead and replace yours. Where we are heading, I think we are going to need them before all this is over. I heard that the Germans are putting up a pretty big fight to retake that bridge."

"Thanks, doc," Jansen said as he grabbed the supplies from O'Connor's bag.

The two young soldiers got up and let the medic take over working on the injured man. They looked over at their squad. The men were all just sitting around smoking cigarettes and waiting for Collins to return with their orders. Jansen and Ellison returned and joined their fellow soldiers.

Jansen looked down at his hands. They were covered with blood. He checked the dressing on his injured hand. Luckily, his wound had stayed clean, but still, he felt it would be a good idea to change the bandages when he got a chance.

Jansen and Ellison sat down in the field near the other member of their squad. Jansen began digging through his combat pack for bandages so he could change the dressing on his hand. When he removed the dressing, he could see that his hand had stopped bleeding where the medic had stitched him up yesterday, and the wound was healing nicely.

After Jansen was finished replacing the dressing on his hand he looked up and saw Ellison sitting quietly, smoking a cigarette. Jansen decided to let his friend process the morning's events on his own.

Before their column had been strafed by the Stukas, Jansen was already feeling anxious, thinking about what lay ahead of him in the coming hours. Then there was the air attack. And finally, they had to deal with the man with the wounded shoulder. Jansen just wanted something to take his mind off things for a while.

Jansen pulled out a cigarette, lit it, and let the smoke fill his lungs. He looked over at Ellison. His friend was just sitting there quietly. Jansen knew that Ellison would be back to his normal self before long. Tim was a different person in combat, and it usually took a while for his friend to switch gears in these situations. Jansen decided to leave his friend alone and give him some space.

Meanwhile, the rest of the squad was just hanging out waiting for Sergeant Collins to return, occasionally looking to the sky to see if the Stukas that had attacked them wanted to return and try to finish what they had started.

It was about nine o'clock when Sergeant Collins returned with instructions   from   the   company   CO.

CHAPTER FIVE

MECKENHEIM

March 8, 1945
0830 Hours

"Listen up!" Collins started as he addressed the squad, "Captain Horn wants us to march the rest of the way to Meckenheim. It is a three-mile march and we only have about an hour before we need to be there so we can be on-time to link up with the rest of the regiment. We need you all to meet up at the captain's jeep, and we will move out from there."

Collins left the squad to relay the orders to the next squad in his platoon. Parker got up and announced, "You heard the man, get up, and rally over by the CO's jeep."

The men got to their feet, collected their gear, and started making their way down the road to the head of the column where Captain Horn was standing next to his jeep talking with his driver and radio operator. As they were walking Harrison came up to Jansen.

"Hey Jansen, hand me those satchels and you take the Browning for the first part of the march."

Jansen knew that this march probably was not going to be long enough for the two machine gunners to switch off carrying the machine gun. But he decided not to argue.

"Sure, here they are," Jansen said as he took the two satchels full of ammo off his shoulders and handed them to Harrison. Harrison took the ammo and handed the machine gun to Jansen. Jansen took the weapon and lifted it onto his shoulder. And just like that, all was as it should be, the Replacement was carrying the large, ungainly weapon, and the Veteran was carrying the ammo in two easy to carry satchels.

The men of Mike Company converged on Captain Horn's jeep. Horn addressed the men, "I'm not going to waste your time. Colonel Willingham, our regimental commander, is expecting us in Meckenheim in an hour. I've talked to your platoon sergeants and they all know the location of the assembly area for the regiment in Meckenheim. Stay on this road and try to keep close to some sort of cover or concealment in case some other Nazi pilot decides to attack us. Let's line up and move out."

The men of Mike Company formed a long line along the road, staying in their respective platoons. There was not much cover or concealment along the route except for farm buildings and the occasional tree. As the men walked along on the side of the road there was still a steady stream of military vehicles full of troops traveling on the road. The trucks they had been in when their convoy was attacked were being checked for damage. Those trucks would make their way to Meckenheim by another route.

The cold morning air was now less biting. For the first time all morning, Jansen was beginning to feel truly warm as he marched with the rest of the men from Mike Company along what would normally have been an unimportant road in the German countryside.

He started by balancing the machine gun on his right shoulder, steadying the huge barrel with his right hand. It was not long before the receiver and barrel started to dig into his shoulder, and he switched the weapon over to his other shoulder. There simply was no easy way to carry the heavy machine gun.

Jansen's unit was marching in a single file. Jansen was marching between Ellison and Harrison. Even though Jansen wanted to complain to Ellison about having to carry the thirty-one-pound weapon, he thought better of it after realizing that Harrison would most likely overhear him complaining. Jansen was quite sure that Harrison would lay into him if that happened. Besides, Jansen was usually not one to complain anyway.

Ellison slowed down a bit and turned to talk to Jansen, "One good thing about all this marching around, my feet are finally starting to warm up."

"Yeah, I know what you mean, I am finally starting to warm up too," answered Jansen.

"Oh, don't get me wrong, I'm still not warm! I am more of a Californian now and am just not used to cold weather anymore. I am looking forward to getting back home where the weather stays pretty warm most of the year. I'm not like you South Dakota types who are used to the cold."

Jansen's mind recalled the harsh winters he endured while living in South Dakota and could remember how extremely cold he and his family would get during the winters there. It was especially bad growing up there during the Depression when everything was scarce, including warm clothes.

"Yeah, this isn't as cold as where I grew up," Jansen recalled, "Did I ever tell you the story about the bet I made with my brother?"

Ellison stopped for a second and said, "Everybody, listen up! Jansen has a story he wants to tell!"

Of course when you are marching in a single file column and everyone is observing a correct distance from the man in front of them, even if you shout something stupid, at most only about three or four guys can hear you. Ellison had only raised his voice a little over normal talking volume, so his comment did not draw any unwanted attention.

Jansen knew Ellison was just making fun of his quiet nature, "Do you want to hear the story or not smart ass?" Jansen replied laughing.

"Okay, Jansen, sorry. I guess now is the time for me to shut up and let you talk."

"When we were growing up, we would never wear socks in the summertime. We only started wearing our socks when it would start to get cold. So, one year my brother and I decided to make a bet to see who could go the longest without wearing socks as the weather started to turn cold," Jansen began.

Jansen moved the machine gun he was carrying over to his other shoulder and continued with his story, "We started the bet in September, and everything was going well for the first month or so. But as November approached the temperatures began to drop fast. Neither my brother nor I would give in. Even though we were freezing we wouldn't start wearing our socks. So, one day the two of us went down to the river and I got so cold that I passed out. When I came too, my brother and I walked back to my house and I put on socks and I decided that winning the bet wasn't worth it."

"That was a great story Jansen, but you should probably try to come up with a better ending."

Jansen did not understand Ellison's critique of his story and asked, "What do you mean?"

Ellison was a real raconteur, which was the main part of his charm, "Well, the ending is pretty boring and falls kind of flat. My guess is that in real life there were some interesting details that you left out. Like, what happened when you fainted. Did you fall in the river? Maybe you fell into the water, were swept away by the current, and your brother had to jump into the river to save you."

"The only problem with that is that none of what you just said happened," Jansen replied. This illustrated perfectly that Jansen and Ellison were fundamentally different people, especially when it came to things like this. Jansen was exceedingly honest, maybe to a fault, and not much of a storyteller. Ellison on the other hand could take an ordinary story from his life, and just by the way he told it could spin it into a wildly entertaining tale. Plus, Ellison was not averse to embellishing his stories with purely invented elements for dramatic effect.

Ellison knew that teaching Jansen how to tell a good story might be a lost cause, but he figured it was worth a shot anyway, "The point is that I am pretty sure that your story is way more interesting than it came across when you told it. You could put in facts about what kind of person your brother was like. Was he super stubborn and that is why he won the bet? What other things happened to the two of you in the days before you fainted at the river? How did your brother react to you fainting, knowing that you fainted because of a silly bet you had taken with him? Do you understand what I am getting at?"

Jansen could see what his friend was trying to tell him, but the pragmatic side of him said that trying to turn himself into a raconteur might be a lost cause. "I see what you mean, but I'm just not sure that I have it in me to be some great storyteller," Jansen said as he lowered his machine gun off of his shoulder and began to carry it by its handle.

"That may be true," said Ellison with a tone of understanding in his voice, "but let me ask you to do two things; first, try to think about how to add details to your stories to make them more interesting, and second, don't stop telling stories, even if you and everyone else think they are boring."

"Deal," Jansen replied.

"Did I ever tell you the story about the time my brother and I fixed up an old Model T?" Ellison asked.

"No, I don't think I remember that one."

"Okay," Ellison started, "my brother and I were walking back from school one day and we saw this old Model T truck just sitting out in a field with weeds growing up under it. So, we went to the farmhouse near where we saw the truck and knocked on the door. And an older lady answered the door. We asked her about the truck. She said that it belonged to her husband who had recently died and that it didn't run. So, my brother and I told her that we could haul it to the scrap metal drive for her since it was just rusting away and collecting weeds. That was a bit of a fib because what we wanted to do is to try and get that old truck running again. She agreed to let us haul it away for her, so we went home and asked our dad if it was okay with him if we took our two horses over to the widow's farm to tow away the truck. My dad agreed and we took the horses over to the widow's farm."

"So, your family still used horses?" asked Jansen.

"Yeah, the horses were the only livestock my dad didn't have to sell when he lost his farm. What about your dad's farm? Did your dad still use horses too?" Ellison inquired.

"Yup," Jansen answered.

"So anyway, where was I? Oh, yeah, so my brother and I took a team of horses over to the old lady's farm and hooked them up to this old Model T. Lucky for us the tires still held air and we only needed to pump them up a little to get the truck rolling again. We then used the horses to tow the truck down the road. After we got it back to my dad's place my brother and I spent all of our spare time working on that old truck, scrounging parts from wherever we could find them. And eventually, after a lot of hard work, we got that old truck running again."

"Wow! That sounds like a good story," Jansen interjected.

"I haven't even gotten to the interesting part," replied Ellison.

"So, my brother and I would take turns driving that old truck around town, acting like a couple of big shots. Anyway, one night I drove that old truck into town, and I meet a friend of mine from school, and he's just walking along the side of the road. So, I pull up alongside him and ask if he wanted a ride. It was getting dark and he didn't want to have to walk home in the dark, so he agreed and hopped into the truck. As we are driving along, we get into this really good conversation about girls and how far each of us had gone with the members of the opposite sex. And when we pulled up to his house the conversation was just getting good, so I just parked the truck and turned off its headlights. By the looks of it, his family had already gone to bed, because we couldn't see any lights on in the house. So after about half an hour or so, our conversation had wrapped up and we decided to go inside his house for a bit. We walk up to the front door to go inside and it's locked. We thought that was kind of weird, so we walked around the house to the back door and that door is locked too. At this point, my friend tells me that his family never locks the doors at night, and never ever locks the back door. So now my friend starts banging on the door asking to be let in. When his family heard his voice, his brother finally unlocked the door and they turned on the lights, and there was his mom holding a loaded shotgun. What I didn't know is that his dad was out of town and his mom was home alone with the kids. So, when an unknown truck showed up on their property and parked outside their house for half an hour, she naturally got nervous. She thought that we must have been there to rob the place or something and I guess she was about to open fire when she finally realized that it was her son and his idiot friend that had been parked outside her house."

"That story would have been hilarious if your friend's mom had shot the two of you in the butt with rock salt or something," Jansen said laughing.

"Don't laugh, that almost happened. Besides the shotgun wasn't loaded with rock salt, she had buckshot in that thing. If she had unloaded on us, I probably wouldn't be here to tell the story. But I have to admit that getting shot with rock salt would be a good addition to the story. I will remember that the next time I tell it. But, just to be clear, as I just told it, that story was one hundred percent true," Ellison explained.

At this point, the company picked up the pace a little to make sure that they would make it to Meckenheim in time. So, Jansen and Ellison decided to curtail their conversation and focus on the march.

Mike Company marched along the road without incident, and as they got closer to Meckenheim, they saw more traffic on the road. They even met other units from their regiment that were also on the road marching toward their regimental assembly area.

Jansen and Ellison had not talked much after their company

picked up to pace. It was just too hard to hold a conversation and march quickly at the same time. This was especially true for Jansen. He was still moving the machine gun into different carrying positions, but nothing he did seemed to help. It seemed as though the Browning machine gun was determined to make Jansen as miserable as possible during this march.

Just about the time Jansen was about ready to give up and ask Harrison if he could trade with him, he saw the assembly area off in the distance. Jansen was exhausted already, but he figured he could tough it out a little longer. Besides, he did not want to give Harrison another reason to think that he was not a good soldier. Jansen also figured that even if he did ask to switch off carrying the Browning, there was still a good chance that Harrison would simply refuse to make the trade.

Soon Mike Company made it to the assembly area. It was 0930 hours. The men had made the march in a little under an hour. Captain Horn found an open area in a field outside the city of Meckenheim for his company and then left in his jeep to get instructions from the 311th Regimental Headquarters as to what they were to do next.

Jansen found a dry piece of grass and sat down in the field. He extended the bipods on the machine gun to keep it off the ground and placed it next to him. He did not want to get the machine gun dirty, undoing all the work he had done to clean it the previous day. Jansen then laid down on the grass next to the machine gun. He was exhausted.

Ellison sat down next to his friend as Jansen closed his eyes. The combination of walking back from sick-call yesterday, getting up at 0330 hours this morning, and now this march were all beginning to take a toll on Jansen.

"Hey, Jansen, don't fall asleep. Parker and Collins will definitely not be happy if they catch you sleeping," Ellison said.

"Don't worry, I'm just resting my eyes," Jansen answered.

Ellison knew his friend just needed a bit of a break, so he left him alone.

After the march, Jansen finally was not cold anymore. His legs were tired, and his back and feet were sore. He knew he would not be able to rest for too long before he would draw the ire of Parker, Collins, or one of the Veterans. Jansen wanted to get up on his own before that happened, so he only laid on the grass for a little bit before he sat up. If he were somewhat vertical, he figured that he would be left alone.

As Jansen sat on the outskirts of Meckenheim, he looked out at his regiment's assembly area. He had never seen his entire regiment in one place before and it was quite a sight; three battalions, thirteen companies, and almost four thousand men, all in one place, and all were there for the same reason, to cross a little known bridge at the city of Remagen.

Before long, Captain Horn returned from the 311th Regimental Headquarters. Their company was to load up onto trucks and move out to Remagen at 1000 hours. Jansen and the other soldiers of Mike Company would only have a few more minutes before they would be heading out again to a small town on banks of the Rhine River where the battle for a little-known railway bridge was underway.

CHAPTER SIX

REMAGEN

March 8, 1945
0945 Hours

After Captain Horn returned from his meeting with the top brass, he called together his platoon leaders and platoon sergeants. Before long Sergeant Collins came over to Jansen's squad and told the men to get into formation.

Jansen pulled himself to his feet, every part of his body was either sore or tired or both. He began walking with Ellison and the rest of his squad over to where their company was forming up.

Sergeant Parker began barking orders to get the rest of the squad to the company formation, "Come on ladies, on your feet."

The men quickly got into formation and soon they were ready to hear from their commander.

"Good morning, men," Captain Horn began, "we will be loading up onto trucks in a few minutes. The plan is to roll out at 1000 hours. Each battalion will take a different route to manage congestion on the roads leading to Remagen. As you can probably guess, right now everyone in the American Army is trying to get to Remagen, so the traffic on the roads is going to be pretty heavy. Once we get to Remagen, we will link up again with the first and second battalions and wait for our turn to cross the bridge. Since we will be traveling by different roads, we will need to form up with the rest of the third battalion. Platoon leaders, you will march your men over to the third battalion assembly area."

After the men were dismissed, Collins proceeded to march the platoon over to the assembly area. The men were quiet as they marched in formation. The rest of third battalion wasn't far from where Mike Company had assembled at the end of their march. Soon Jansen could see that the trucks were already lining up to receive the men of his battalion.

While marching over to the trucks Jansen turned to Harrison and asked, "Hey Harrison, could we trade off carrying the M1919 and the ammo?"

"Sure, I can take the machine gun, let's make the switch when we load up into the trucks," Harrison said.

Jansen was grateful that Harrison agreed to take the machine gun. Jansen decided that Harrison took it because it was unlikely that they would be forced to march again as they had on the road to Meckenheim.

Soon their company had joined the men of third battalion. It was almost 1000 hours. Jansen handed the machine gun to Harrison, "Here you go," he said as he took the satchels with the ammo belts from Harrison.

As Harrison took the machine gun from Jensen he thought about saying something like, "You owe me for taking this off your hands," but thought better of it considering that Jansen had just finished carrying the weapon on the forced-march after the Stuka attack. For Jansen's part, he was glad to be rid of that heavy weapon for a while and was a little surprised that Harrison did not have a snide remark for him about the exchange.

Sergeant Collins knew he did not have much time to get his men loaded into the waiting trucks, "Okay men, load up onto the trucks and keep the platoon together."

The men made their way over to the trucks and started climbing in. Jansen got into the back of one truck with other men from his squad. Harrison was right behind him. Knowing how hard it is to climb into the back of a deuce-and-a-half while carrying the machine gun Jansen said, "Hey, Harrison, hand up the Browning." Harrison handed the machine gun to Jansen and climbed into the back of the truck. Jansen then handed the weapon back to his fellow machine gunner.

"Thanks, Jansen."

"Don't mention it," Jansen replied as he looked for a seat.

Ellison was one of the next soldiers to climb into the truck, he found a seat across from Jansen. Soon Sergeant Parker crawled into the back of the truck and decided to sit right next to Jansen. Even though he had spent a fair amount of time sleeping on the ground in less than ideal conditions, Jansen could not help feeling a little uneasy sitting next to Parker. Jansen was convinced that he would get either lice or fleas or something worse from Parker on the truck ride to Remagen. Jansen just sat there quietly and tried not to think about it.

It seemed like the regiment had a lot of trucks to transport the men to Remagen. On this ride only a few men in Jansen's company had to sit on the floorboards of the trucks, Jansen was glad it was not him this time.

At around ten o'clock the truck in which Jansen was riding began to move.

"I guess this is it," said Ellison nervously.

"We'll know what this hubbub is all about soon enough," said Jansen as he fidgeted with his web gear.

"Nobody cares what you two morons think," snapped Parker, "So I would suggest that you just shut up. Understand?"

"Yes, sergeant," replied Jansen. Ellison just sat there and did not say anything.

Jansen knew Parker well enough to understand that Parker would get anxious, just like everyone else, as they were going into combat. And Parker's way of dealing with it was to throw his rank around and lash out. Jansen being a Replacement and a buck private knew his place and decided to just keep his mouth shut.

Parker's outburst made everyone in the truck uneasy. So, for quite a while after Parker laid into Jansen and Ellison everyone in the truck was pretty quiet. The only ones who dared talk at all were some of the Veterans.

The deuce-and-a-half lumbered along the road leading to Remagen. Traffic was heavy on the roads, so the convoy was making slow progress toward its destination. Things were quiet in the back of the truck as the convoy rolled through the open farmland, passing through the occasional farming village.

Jansen needed something to take his mind off the situation. He was already feeling nervous about going back to the front lines and Parker's outburst only made matters worse. He took out a cigarette and lit it. Most of the men in the truck were smoking, probably for the same reason. Jansen looked out at the countryside and tried to think of his farming community back home in South Dakota.

The convoy was making painfully slow progress and seemed to be crawling along. Remagen was only eleven miles away from Meckenheim, so it should have been a short trip by vehicle. But with the heavy traffic and constant stopping and starting, the trip was taking longer than it should. The slow pace began to wear on Jansen's nerves.

Before long, the men could begin to hear the battle. The first thing they could hear was the dull "thud" of the German artillery guns firing off in the distance. These would be the German guns at Erpeler Ley, which were located on a plateau on the east side of the Rhine River overlooking the river and the town of Remagen. As they got closer, they could hear the sound of the artillery shells and bombs exploding near the bridge.

Once the men began hearing the battle that was raging less than a mile from their position, things got even quieter in the back of the truck. The soldiers stopped talking and sat in silence as the trucks passed by the farms and cottages on the outskirts of Remagen.

Just before eleven o'clock, the convoy reached Remagen. An MP in the road directed the convoy to the location in the city where the third battalion would need to go to link up with the rest of the regiment.

Even though the city of Remagen was well within the range of the German artillery guns on top of Erpeler Ley, it was safe for the Americans to assemble in the town for a couple of reasons. First, the buildings of the town offered concealment from the German artillery spotters on the plateau of Erpeler Ley. And second, the Germans were still trying to destroy the bridge and they were focusing their fire there and on the American units on the east side of the Rhine that were fighting to expand the bridgehead. This meant that instead of shelling the town in hopes of hitting something by chance, the German guns were firing where they knew it could do the most damage to the American advance across the Rhine.

The convoy worked its way into the city of Remagen. Jensen could see American troops and vehicles everywhere. The large lumbering trucks worked their way to the assembly area for the 311th Infantry Regiment. Some members of the 311th were already there milling about on the narrow streets. These men had to move out of the way when the convoy pulled up. One by one the trucks unloaded their human cargo and continued down the narrow streets, slowly making their way out of the city on their way to pick up more soldiers.

The truck Jansen was in came to a stop. Jansen waited his turn as other members of his unit made their way to the back of the truck and jumped out. Jansen walked to the back of the truck and jumped onto the street, his boots landing on the hard cobblestone with a dull thud. Ellison jumped out of the back of the truck right behind him.

The sounds of war were more prevalent now and the two men could hear the guns of Erpler Ley, the sirens from the Stuka dive bombers attacking the bridge, the American anti-aircraft guns, and they could even hear the sound of machine-gun fire from across the river. It brought where they were and what they were about to do into clear focus. There was no doubt, this would be the most intense fighting these two farm kids had experienced so far.

Jensen looked over at his friend. There was a seriousness in Ellison's face that made the moment seem even more grave and caused a pit to grow in Jansen's stomach.

There was plenty of noise, but almost none of it was coming from the soldiers who were waiting their turn to cross the Ludendorff Bridge at Remagen. The noise was coming from every direction; the German attacks on the bridge, the constant flow of military vehicles on the streets of Remagen, and finally the sound of soldiers being dropped off and then picked up as the American Army prepared to expand the bridgehead.

Even though there was a brief break for the men of Jansen's unit, most of the men couldn't rest. Jansen and Ellison sat in silence, enjoying the brief break, but still nervously thinking about what lay ahead.

The two men found a place to sit down and relax. Since Jansen had joined the unit, his platoon had not had a platoon leader. This was because Captain Horn had been promoted from platoon leader of Jansen's platoon to company commander just before Jansen joined the unit. Jansen still had not learned what had happened to the previous company commander. The Veterans did not like talking to the Replacements in general and definitely did not like talking about members of the unit that had been lost in combat.

The absence of a platoon leader did make life a little easier for the men of Jansen's platoon. For Jansen, it meant that he did not have an officer messing with him on a regular basis. It is important to note here that Jansen was just an eighteen-year-old kid who had never picked up a razor before he joined the Army, so shaving was not a normal part of his daily routine. And since he did not have much of a beard yet, he could usually go a few days without shaving before anyone would notice.

This morning Jansen had planned to shave because it had been a few days, but getting roused from bed and mobilized for combat at zero dark thirty had nixed those plans. It was now becoming clear that he needed a shave. Jansen was not worried because they were in the field, and there were different standards between life in garrison and life in combat.

Jansen and Ellison were sitting and waiting for their unit to load up on trucks and cross the bridge when Lieutenant Wilson from one of the other platoons in Jansen's company walked up to the two young soldiers. Jansen and Ellison came to attention and saluted the young officer.

"At ease soldiers," was the terse response from the lieutenant. He looked at Jansen, "son when was the last time you shaved?"

"About three days ago sir," Jansen replied.

"It looks like you're due for another shave private," Wilson replied.

"I suppose so, sir," Jansen replied.

"I know we won't be loading up on the trucks to cross the bridge for at least an hour. You have plenty of time to find some water and get that peach fuzz shaved before we jump off."

Jansen's face looked honestly confused. He had always kept his shaving gear in his footlocker and had never thought of taking it out into the field. The idea of shaving in combat had honestly never come up.

"Sir," Jansen responded, "I don't have my shaving gear with me in my combat pack."

"Really, private!" Wilson replied. Jansen could tell the LT was getting irritated, "And where is your shaving gear?"

"I keep it in my footlocker sir."

"Why don't you have it with you?" at this point, Wilson was becoming even more irritated.

"I thought we weren't expected to shave while we were in the field," Jansen sheepishly replied. He had not been dressed down by an officer before. Also, he had never gotten in trouble for something that seemed so trivial.

Lieutenant Wilson was now almost yelling at Jansen, "Do you know that most casualties in combat are hygiene-related? I'll be back in thirty minutes, and I expect to see you clean-shaven when I return, understand?"

"Yes, sir," Jansen replied. As the lieutenant stormed away, Jansen had no idea what he was going to do to get a shave before the young officer returned.

"Jansen, don't worry about the LT, I keep my shaving kit in my combat pack, you can borrow mine if you want," Ellison said as he began to dig through his gear.

"Ah! Found it!" Ellison cried and he pulled out his shaving kit.

Jansen found a faucet, took off his helmet, filled it with ice-cold water, and began the process of shaving his sorry excuse for a beard, on the streets of Remagen on a cold day in early March. As he was shaving near the corner of his mouth, the razor hit a rough patch of Jansen's face, and the blade nicked his skin. A single drop of blood fell from his face into the water of Jansen's helmet. The crimson drop quickly dispersed into the mixture of soap and water.

Jansen finished shaving, turned on the nearby faucet, and splashed the cold water onto his face and was relieved to see that the cut was not bad and had already stopped bleeding.

As Jansen cleaned out his helmet and returned it to his head, he gathered his friend's shaving kit and handed it to him, "Here Ellison, thanks for letting me borrow that by the way."

"You look a full five percent better than you did before you shaved. The LT should be happy," Ellison said as he took his shaving kit and returned it to his combat pack.

That little diversion helped to break some of the tension. Jansen and Ellison began to chat about unimportant things to pass the time.

Before long, Lieutenant Wilson returned. He was surprised that Jansen had been able to find shaving gear. After Wilson inspected Jansen's face, he made some vague warnings and then left the soldiers alone.

From where they were sitting, Jansen and Ellison could see the other members of their squad sitting or lying on various items in the Remagen street doing their best to relax and prepare mentally for what lay ahead of them. Some of the men were nervously chatting, some were just relaxing, and others were taking the time to write letters home. Most of them were having a few last cigarettes while they still had the time.

Jansen could see Harrison with the Browning machine gun, he was checking it to ensure that it was fully functional and ready for combat.

Jansen and Ellison were both sitting on the cobblestone street in nervous silence, smoking, and enjoying their last few moments before getting the call to cross the bridge. Jansen could see Sergeant Collins approach the squad. This must mean that it is about time to make the crossing. Jansen kept reminding himself that the apprehension he was feeling now was probably nothing compared to what the men felt just before they landed at the beaches of Normandy during the D-Day invasion.

"Okay men," Collins yelled, "the regiment will begin loading up on trucks and crossing the Rhine. We will be assembling on one of the main roads and will load up on trucks as they come back from running soldiers over the bridge. We will be crossing one company at a time, so we will be the last company from this regiment to cross. We need to march over to where the trucks will pick us up, so let's grab our gear and move out!"

The platoon gathered up their gear and marched over to where the entire 311th Infantry Regiment was lined up. Each company in the Regiment awaited its turn to cross over the last major physical barrier separating the Allies from the heart of Nazi Germany.

CHAPTER SEVEN

THE BRIDGE

March 8, 1945
1200 Hours

Once Mike Company reached its final assembly area before crossing the Rhine River, Jansen could see all thirteen companies of the 311th Infantry Regiment lined up and waiting to load up on the trucks that would take them across the bridge. Collins instructed his platoon to stay together as they waited their turn.

The assembly area was on a larger street that was more open than the narrow streets where they had just been waiting. This meant that Jansen could see and hear more of the battle than he could before. Every once in a while, he could see and hear a Ju-87 Stuka trying to bomb the bridge.

The morning was still overcast and cold. And since Mike Company's road march had ended hours earlier, the cold was beginning to penetrate through the layers of clothing Jansen was wearing. He began to feel cold. Jansen did not want to be waiting in the cold, but what he had to look forward to when the waiting was over was even worse. He would be back to the front lines fighting a determined German foe on the other side of the Rhine.

As Jansen looked down the street at the rest of his regiment, he could see that some of the first platoons were being briefed by black officers from the transportation unit. This unit was operating the trucks that were taking the soldiers across the Ludendorff Bridge.

Growing up in a Dutch farming community in South Dakota and then being drafted into the Army that was segregated, Jansen had never really seen very many black folks in his young life. Jansen watched as a group of young black officers made their way through the assembly area briefing the various companies in Jansen's regiment.

Eventually, one of the black officers came over to Jansen's platoon. Sergeant Collins called for the men to gather around so that they could hear the briefing. A young officer stepped forward and addressed the men.

"Good morning soldiers, my name is Lieutenant Lewis. Our unit will be responsible for transporting you all safely across the Ludendorff Bridge. German artillery and Stukas are still trying to take down the bridge, but I can tell you that for you there is little danger from those attacks. The American anti-aircraft guns are doing a fairly good job of preventing the Stukas from getting too close to the bridge, so they have not been able to get close enough to hit the bridge yet. And the artillery has not been much of an issue either. So far, all the artillery rounds and bombs have landed in the river. When that happens, the shrapnel isn't traveling fast enough to do very much damage. So just remember to keep your steel pot on and stay low and you should be fine."

Lieutenant Lewis continued, "Our job, is to get your regiment over the bridge as quickly as possible and then come back here to pick up more soldiers. So once we get to the Erpel side of the bridge we will need you all to offload as quickly as possible so the truck drivers can make it back across the bridge in time to pick up the next group of soldiers. Also, listen to your drivers, they know what they are doing, and they have been moving through enemy fire all day. They will do whatever they can to get you to the other side of the river safely. That is all."

With that, the young officer left the men of Jansen's platoon and rejoined his fellow officers as they were wrapping up their briefings with the other platoons of Mike Company. The transportation officers were now done briefing the 311th Infantry Regiment.

Collins told the men to stay together. The men of his platoon were mostly standing now since there was almost no room to sit. The soldiers were in one tightly packed group as they waited their turn in line.

Jansen could see trucks arriving and picking up the first groups of soldiers from his regiment. He looked at his watch, it was 1215 hours on Thursday, March 8th, 1945. Jansen's regiment had officially started crossing the Rhine River into Germany. His regiment was about to join the fight at the Battle of Remagen.

In a way, Jansen was glad that he was being forced to stand. Standing, Jansen reasoned, was a more active position than just sitting, and so it would help keep him a little warmer. As he stood there, Jansen stamped his feet and rubbed his hands, trying to stay warm.

Jansen was tall enough and close enough to the edge of the group to look down the street and see almost his entire regiment. He watched as the trucks would pull up in front of the huge group of soldiers, stop, wait for the soldiers to pile into the back of the truck, and then take off toward the river. It was kind of like a huge, choreographed assembly line.

Before long, Jansen recognized that some of the same trucks and drivers he had noticed earlier were returning to the area to pick up more soldiers. Jansen could not help but admire the black truck drivers, dutifully driving into the crosshairs of the German artillery and Stuka attacks time and again, without rest or complaint.

As Jansen was watching the trucks picking up the men of his regiment and taking off toward the river, he noticed two German men that were walking down the street in front of them. They looked to be in their early thirties and able-bodied. They were saying something in German. Sergeant Parker, who was near, could hear the two men talking.

"Do you see those two guys?" Parker said, "I'll bet they were left over here when the German Army bugged out over the bridge. They are probably German soldiers left here to spot for their artillery!"

Jansen was close enough to the two men to hear what they were saying, he turned to Parker, "I wouldn't worry about those two guys sarge."

"Oh really, Jansen! And what would you know about it?"

"Unless they are putting on a really good show, they are just two factory workers who live in Erpel and work here in Remagen. They are wondering how they are going to get home since the bridge has been closed to civilian traffic. Besides, they were looking for a street sign because they weren't exactly sure where they were," Jansen replied.

"Hopefully, you are right about that," Parker replied, "But I also think that it is weird that you speak German. What are you, some kind of a Kraut?"

"Not at all, sergeant," Jansen said, "I speak Dutch, but it is close enough to German that I could understand most of what those two Krauts were saying."

Jansen had decided to throw in the term "Kraut" to describe the two German men because he figured that next Parker was probably going to question his loyalty. And he thought that using a derogatory term for Germans would cut off that line of attack. His plan worked because Parker then dropped the subject and left him alone.

As Jansen was feeling good that his conversation with the brash New Yorker had ended without incident, he looked up and could see Sergeant Collins walking over to their platoon.

Collins walked into the center of the area where his platoon was gathered and said, "I just heard from the captain that it is going to take a least a couple of hours for the entire regiment to make it across the bridge. So, since we have some time on our hands, the captain wants us to eat lunch. We have a long day ahead of us, so you boys better eat up while you have the chance."

Jansen took off his web gear and began digging through his combat pack for his K-rations. Jansen removed the meal then began looking for a place to sit down and eat. He found a spot and soon Ellison came over and sat near him.

Ellison began talking almost as soon as he sat down, "You know Jansen, that there are probably guys from 1st Battalion that are eating their K-rations right now too, only they are on the other side of the Rhine."

"I suppose you're right. We'll be with them soon enough I suppose," Jansen said as he opened one of the cans and began eating.

Ellison was working on opening his cans as well, "You do know why they call this stuff SPAM, don't you?" he said as he opened the tin can containing weird looking meat.

"Actually, I haven't heard that one yet," answered Jansen as he ate a spoonful of baked beans.

"SPAM stands for, Scientifically Preserved Army Meat," Ellison said with a chuckle as he finished opening the last tin of his K-rations.

"It wouldn't surprise me if that was true," said Jansen. Eating cold K-rations on a cold day, as he was waiting to go into combat was not Jansen's idea of a nice meal. But he was glad that he had Ellison with him to help him keep his mind from worrying about where they were headed and what they were about to do. The sounds of the battle were constantly in the background, but for a few moments, Jansen was not a private in the Army waiting to go into combat, he was just a guy having lunch with a friend.

When the two had finished their meal, they cleaned off their mess kits and then took a smoke break. They watched as the trucks continued to pick up soldiers from their regiment to ferry them across the bridge to the other side of the Rhine. The trucks were loaded up with about 25 to 30 men at a time, which was near the maximum capacity of the two and a half-ton trucks.

As they were watching their regiment get smaller and smaller as more of their fellow soldiers were being carried away by the military trucks, Jansen noticed a truck that was coming back from one of its many trips across the bridge with smoke coming out from under its hood. It pulled over on the side of the street, not far from where Jansen and Ellison were standing.

Once the truck stopped, two drivers hopped out and opened the hood of the truck. Partly out of boredom and partly out of curiosity, Jansen and Ellison walked over to the stranded truck.

The two drivers were looking at the engine as Jansen and Ellison approached. Jansen could see two bullet holes in the truck's hood which had been flipped open and was now leaning against the cab. One of the drivers looked at the two approaching infantrymen.

"What do you two want?" he asked as he turned his attention back to the engine of his truck.

"Oh nothing," Ellison replied. "We were wondering if you needed any help."

"Nah, there isn't much we can do at this point," the driver said, "We were strafed by a Stuka as we were coming back across the bridge. Normally the Stuka pilots are so worried about getting hit by anti-aircraft fire that they have a hard time lining up for a good shot. This guy must have gotten lucky, he put a hole in the engine block, and now it's leaking oil."

"Well," said Ellison, "there isn't much you can do about that. I thought the problem might be something easy to fix. How many trips have you made so far?"

"I can't say for sure," the driver said as he hopped off the truck's bumper and onto the cobblestone street,. "We've been running non-stop for about ten hours already, and it doesn't look like they are going to give us a break any time soon."

"It must be tough driving on the bridge out in the open like that, having to deal with the artillery and Stuka attacks," Jansen interjected.

"The amount of fire we take comes in waves, so it isn't like we have to deal with it all the time. Besides, it's just part of the job," the driver replied, "Hey, thanks for offering to help, but we are going to have to get back to our unit and let our LT know that this truck is out of commission for now. It was nice talking to you two, keep your heads down when you get across the river."

With that, the two black soldiers started walking back to their unit, and Jansen and Ellison walked over to rejoin the rest of their platoon. The men of Mike Company were not done waiting yet. They would not begin to load up on the trucks for another two hours.

During that time Jansen and Ellison spent most of their time just watching the trucks constantly driving into the area with an empty truck, loading up with 25 to 30 men, and then leaving the area to carry their load of soldiers across the bridge.

As more of the men of the 311th Infantry Regiment left on the trucks to be taken across the Ludendorff Bridge, space opened up for other units to come into the area. Soon another unit was lined up behind the last few companies of Jansen's regiment.

Jansen and the rest of his company were the last soldiers of his unit to board the trucks as they prepared to cross the bridge. It had been almost four hours since Jansen's unit had arrived in Remagen. And now the time had finally come. The long wait was over, and the real work was about to begin.

Two very tired looking drivers pulled up in front of Jansen's platoon. Parker walked around the back of the truck and dropped the tailgate. Jansen climbed into the back of the truck with the rest of his platoon. Again, he paused to help Harrison with the unruly machine gun as Harrison climbed into the truck. Jansen was grateful that his fellow machine gunner had not tried to hand it back off to him in the many hours they were waiting in Remagen. Jansen figured that since they were about to go into combat, Harrison would decide to keep the Browning and do most of the shooting, leaving Jansen the job of feeding ammo into the machine gun when they began fighting.

Soon the truck was loaded, Sergeant Collins banged on the side of the truck to let the drivers know that everyone was loaded up. The truck started to make its way down the street towards the river. The street the truck was driving on came to a tee as it approached the Rhine River. Jansen could see everything now. The bridge loomed large in the distance. Along the river, anti-aircraft batteries were in place to protect the American Army's most valuable prize. As they finally approached the objective that had been the center of so much attention from both the American and German Armies in the last 24 hours, Jansen looked out over the bridge and could see that it was under another attack from a group of Stuka dive bombers.

The truck Jansen was riding in passed by some anti-aircraft guns. The artillery pieces were firing constantly at the slow-moving dive bombers. Unlike the earlier Stuka attack on the convoy on their way to Meckenheim, the planes were not coming in low for a strafing run. This time the planes were diving down toward the bridge from a high altitude. The higher speed meant that the sirens that were attached to the Stuka's landing gear were much louder and higher pitched.

The Germans used the sirens on the Stukas as a psychological weapon against the Allied troops, and in Jansen's opinion, it was having the desired effect. Jansen could feel his stomach tighten as the truck made its way toward the bridge.

Jansen did not like going into combat while being out in the open on the back of a truck. There was nothing he could do except just sit there. Being on the front lines there was always something you could do to improve your chances of survival. But in this situation, he felt powerless; he could not seek cover, return fire, or fortify his position. The only thing he could do is keep his head down and hope for the best.

The other members of Jansen's unit with him in the truck felt the same way. The tension in the air was palpable, the men were unusually quiet, and Jansen could tell that he was not the only person who was feeling uneasy about the crossing.

The truck continued on the road that ran parallel to the river. The sounds of battle rang through the air. Soon they were at the entrance to the bridge. An MP was standing there directing traffic. The man was remarkably calm given the chaotic nature of everything that was going on around him.

As the truck carrying Jansen and the other men from his unit pulled up to the entrance to the bridge, the MP motioned for them to stop. Jansen could see that some trucks were coming over from the Erpel side of the bridge, so until those trucks had passed the bridge would not be open for eastbound traffic.

Several trucks came off of the bridge heading into the town of Remagen and rumbled past the line of trucks now waiting their turn to pass over the bridge and into the area that the Germans had occupied only a few hours earlier. The MP finally motioned for the line of trucks to move forward and directed them onto the bridge.

The trucks pulled onto the main road leading onto the bridge. Jansen could see two large brick towers flanking each side of the entrance to the bridge. The drivers were quickly and deliberately guiding their trucks around obstacles as they moved onto the main part of the bridge. Jansen could see the water of the Rhine River rushing below them.

Jansen looked up; three Stukas were high overhead. The Stukas had already started their dive-bombing run and were lined up on the bridge. Just then he heard an explosion go off near him. An artillery round had landed in the water near the bridge. The sound of the explosion caught Jansen off guard. The men could hear the slow-moving shrapnel clinking as it bounced off the metal of the bridge's supports.

Collins called out, "Is anyone hit?"

His question was met with silence from his men. That was a good sign.

Jansen refocused his attention on the Stuka dive bombers as they were diving and getting closer to the bridge. The sirens were now louder and higher pitched than earlier, which meant that the planes were picking up speed. The rate of fire from the American anti-aircraft batteries that lined the river intensified. Two of the Stukas dropped their bombs early and peeled off under the onslaught of anti-aircraft fire from the Americans. Jansen could see the bombs fall as the German aircraft pulled up from their dive and flew off.

Both bombs missed their intended target and exploded as they landed in the river. The bombs landed far enough away from Jansen and the others that Collins did not even bother asking if everyone was alright. They could not even hear the shrapnel from the bombs hit the bridge as it had when the artillery round exploded near them earlier.

Besides, all eyes in the truck were fixed on the last Stuka. It was still diving toward them and still had not released its bomb. The men began to wonder if the pilot was also planning to strafe the convoy as well for good measure after he dropped his bomb.

Since there was only one target now for the anti-aircraft gunners to focus on the plane came under intense fire from the American guns. Then one of the American rounds hit the front of the German plane. The plane's engine burst into flames. Jansen could see that the pilot was now flying blind because the smoke from his engine was blowing over the plane's canopy. The German pilot was trying to pull out of the dive, but since he had lost power, it was no use. The plane flew over the convoy of trucks on the bridge and crashed into the river north of the bridge.

As the plane hit the water the bomb the plane was carrying detonated. If there was any chance that the pilot and gunner might have been able to survive the crash, when the bomb exploded, it removed any chance for the crew to make it out alive.

"Burn in Hell you Nazi bastards!" Sergeant Parker yelled from the back of the truck.

After the strafing attack earlier that morning, Jansen had similar feelings to those expressed by his brash, uncouth, squad leader. Jansen knew that the two men in the plane who had just crashed into the Rhine River had been trying to kill him and his fellow soldiers. It was easy to think that they deserved their fate.

Then, without warning, the thought entered Jansen's mind that these two men most likely had loved ones back home that were probably worried about them and were praying for their safe return. In situations like this, Jansen found himself being pulled in two directions.

Jansen had been trained to detach himself from the reality that his job as an infantryman was to kill enemy combatants. But usually, he did not feel anything that could be described as hatred for the enemy, he just performed his duties with a detached, cold indifference. But seeing the deaths of the two German airmen was different. For some reason he had not witnessed the death of two enemy combatants, he had witnessed the death of two fellow human beings. That feeling was something new to him and it made him uncomfortable.

As Jansen was quietly processing the whole situation, the truck continued to move efficiently across the bridge with the other trucks in the column. Jansen could tell that the rate of fire from the German artillery guns on top of Erpeler Ley was dying down. This was just like what the black driver had told him about earlier in Remagen, that the German attacks on the bridge tended to come in waves.

The trucks continued to make their way across the bridge. The two Stukas that were not shot down had broken off their attack and the German artillery had redirected their fire away from the bridge. Soon the trucks made their way past the two brick towers on the far side of the bridge.

The trucks circled around in front of the railway tunnel located at the end of the bridge. That railway tunnel cut into a hill, that hill was Erpeler Ley and was still in German hands. It was the location of the German artillery guns that had been harassing the American's advance into German-held territory. The truck drivers gave the signal for the men to jump out.

Jansen, along with the other soldiers, piled out of the back of the truck as quickly as possible. As soon as the drivers were sure that everyone had been safely delivered across the bridge, they quickly moved out to cross the bridge and drove back to Remagen to pick up more troops.

It was 1530 hours, as Jansen stood on ground that had been occupied by German troops less than 24 hours earlier. Jansen could see Sergeant Collins and some of the platoon leaders talking to another officer near the entrance to the tunnel. Collins returned to where his platoon had been dropped off by the trucks.

Sergeant Collins called his men together, "Okay ladies, we have to regroup with the rest of third battalion in Erpel, just north of here. The rest of the regiment has been waiting for us, so we don't have much time. When we rejoin the rest of our battalion we will be briefed on our assignment. Follow me and move out!"

A wave of fatigue washed over Jansen as he unslung his M1 Carbine rifle and followed Collins along with the rest of his platoon into the German town of Erpel, not knowing what lay ahead.

CHAPTER EIGHT

ERPEL

March 8, 1945
1545 Hours

It was hard to believe that it had been less than twelve hours since Ellison woke Jansen up back in Kalenborn to tell him the unit was moving out to Remagen. Jansen and the rest of his unit had not seen any real combat in the last twelve hours except for being strafed by the Stukas. Even though they still had not been fighting, the last twelve hours had not been easy. And now that they had made it across the Rhine River, the real work would begin.

Jansen and Harrison linked up, now that they were going into combat, these two men would always be together; one man carrying and feeding the machine gun ammo and the other firing the Browning machine gun.

The two soldiers, along with the rest of the company, followed Collins to the outskirts of Erpel. The tiny town looked unassuming. The town of Erpel consisted of small, close-knit houses and narrow streets. The battalion had to meet on the outskirts of the town because there was no way for it to assemble inside the town on its numerous intersecting streets.

As the men approached Erpel, Jansen could see men from his battalion milling about in an open area not too far away. The men of Mike Company joined the rest of the battalion. As he arrived, Jansen noticed a group of jeeps parked in a field next to an old building. Captain Horn was talking with a group of officers from the battalion.

Before long, Captain Horn returned to his company and called together the company's officers and senior enlisted. Sergeant Collins left his men to go over and talk to his company commander. By now the conversation was close enough to Jansen and the rest of the men of Mike Company that they could piece together what their orders were.

Soon Collins returned to his men to fill in any missing details that the men might have missed. "Okay, the regiment has been tasked with taking the city of Bad Honnef. Third battalion will attack the German's right flank, the western side of the city. The catch is that, rather than giving you ladies a leisurely stroll to Bad Honnef, there are still Germans occupying much of this territory, so don't expect this to be a walk in the park, and keep your eyes open. We can't assume that the other members in the 78th Division that have already rolled through this area have completely cleaned out all Germans in the area."

Collins talked briefly with his squad leaders to fill them in on what specifically he wanted from them when the company moved out into the town of Erpel. The narrow streets and the close-knit houses did not give the men of the company much room to maneuver. The company formed two columns as they made their way through the streets.

Jansen and Harrison were marching together, Jansen could see Harrison struggling to carry the machine gun. Ellison was in the column on the other side of the street. Ellison was walking quietly; his normal talkative nature was no longer evident. Jansen had seen this change in his friend before. Combat was not something most people ever get used to, but it seemed to have a more profound effect on his friend.

85

Jansen could see in his friend that combat was harder on Ellison than it was on the other members of his unit. Even compared to the other Replacements, Ellison had a harder time processing the horrible things they had all see up to this point. Jansen thought that this was because his friend was such an outgoing person and when in combat, he had to silence that aspect of his personality. This also would explain Ellison's easy-going and talkative nature that emerged whenever they were not in battle.

By the looks of it, the town was pretty much deserted. Jansen figured that most of the people of the town had fled to nearby areas in advance of the American attack. A few townspeople were peering out of their windows at the American soldiers. From Jansen's position, he could not see any of the locals out in the streets, only American troops and the occasional jeep. Every once in a while, a tank rumbled through the town.

There were plenty of impact craters in the streets to let the men know that earlier, the German guns had dialed in on their current position. But it seemed that at this point, the Nazis were directing their fire further north. Nevertheless, Parker went around to the members of his squad and reminded them to be constantly looking for places to take cover in case the Germans decided to redirect their fire on their squad's position.

Mike Company made steady progress through Erpel. As they moved northwest through the town, they could begin to clearly hear the sounds of the fighting to the north. This only served to heighten their awareness. The soldiers began to proceed more cautiously than before.

Jansen paused to light a cigarette. They were about a mile from where the trucks had dropped them off by the entrance to the railway tunnel. Jansen looked over at Harrison. His fellow machine gunner was carrying the Browning on his shoulder. Jansen had been watching Harrison. They were all getting tired, but hauling around the Browning, was an unpleasant task even under normal circumstances and Jansen could see that the extra work was starting

86

to wear on Harrison.

"Hey Harrison, how you holding up?"

Harrison shifted the machine gun to his other shoulder, "I'm fine."

Even though Jansen had not been with his unit for long, he quickly learned that you never volunteer for anything. This was one of the lessons he learned in basic training that ended up being true in his new unit as well. He knew that if he volunteered to carry the machine gun that he could expect two things to come from that. First, Harrison would lose a little respect for his fellow machine gunner for being stupid enough to volunteer to carry the weapon, and second, Harrison would gladly hand over the weapon and Jansen would be saddled with carrying an unwieldy 31-pound weapon.

Jansen thought that by at least checking in with him he would be letting Harrison know that if he needed to pass off the machine gun, Jansen would be willing to switch off with him and would not complain.

Mike Company had traveled most of the way through the town of Erpel. The sounds of combat were getting closer now as they approached Unkel, the town just north of their position.

Harrison was marching ahead of Jansen, he paused long enough for Jansen to meet up with him.

"Jansen, do you mind taking the Browning for a while?"

Jansen could still remember lugging the machine gun on the three-mile march to Meckenheim after they were strafed by the Stukas. His body was fatigued and he didn't want to take the weapon, but he was impressed that Harrison had lasted as long as he had considering how tired all the men in his company were at this point.

"I can take it for a while," Jansen said as he took the ammo satchels off his shoulders.

The two men traded their loads and resumed their march through the narrow streets.

Jansen decided to use the Browning machine gun's carrying handle while marching.

Mike Company had made it most of the way through Erpel at this point without meeting any German resistance. They were now approaching the border between Erpel and Unkel. The two towns flowed together, but the area between Erpel and Unkel had fewer houses and was more open. This gave the men fewer options for cover and was generally more exposed.

As they approached the end of Erpel, the men came to an open area where there was a fifty-yard gap in the houses between Erpel and Unkel. Jansen and the men in his platoon came up to the open area and stopped. There was almost no cover or concealment in the fifty yards between the towns and even though they could hear that most of the fighting was farther north in the town of Unkel, most everyone understood that it was not a good decision to just cross this area without caution.

Jansen was behind a row of trees and could see almost the entire company, waiting for orders. To his left, he could see Lieutenant Wilson's platoon make its way to the row of trees that separated the town of Erpel from the open field. Wilson and his platoon reached the line of trees and did not notice that the rest of the company had stopped.

Lieutenant Wilson passed the row of trees and started moving into the open field. Some of his men stayed behind the trees, refusing to follow their platoon leader into the open, but some of the greener troops followed him until about a dozen men from his platoon were out in the open.

Jansen heard the whistling sound of an incoming mortar shell and dove for cover. He could hear many other soldiers yelling, "Incoming!" as the rest of the company looked for cover.

About a second later the first mortar shell exploded near Wilson and his men. The Germans still held the high ground northeast of their position. It was obvious now that they had a mortar team in the hills trained on this position.

Wilson and the men that followed him were caught out in the open. Luckily the first round was far enough away that it did not do much damage. There was a slight delay after the first explosion. The Germans were adjusting their aim to get the next few rounds closer to the group of stranded soldiers. The second and third rounds landed much closer to Wilson and his men, some of whom had already run back to the safety of the trees. The rest were crawling back to rejoin the rest of their company and using whatever humps and mounds they could find in the open field to shield them from the mortar explosions.

Lieutenant Wilson was trying to crawl back to the line of trees as quickly as possible and in doing so was not able to keep a low enough profile. A mortar round exploded just about seven yards behind him. He was still about ten yards away from the line of trees and safety.

"I'm hit!" Wilson screamed as he continued to try to crawl back and rejoin his company.

By this time, all the men that were caught in the mortar attack with Wilson had made it back to join the rest of the company. Nobody was severely injured, but the rest of Wilson's platoon was busy taking care of minor injuries from the attack. Meanwhile, Wilson was still stuck out in the open. It was only a matter of time before the Germans adjusted their aim again and finished him off.

Collins was closest to Wilson's position. Jansen could see Collins looking around for a "volunteer." Collins looked at Jansen.

"Jansen, come over here."

Jansen handed the machine gun to Harrison, "I think I'm being volunteered to do something stupid," he said to Harrison just before he crawled over to see his platoon sergeant.

"We are going to go out and get Wilson and carry him back behind cover so the medics can work on him. We will wait for the next mortar round to hit, then we should have a few seconds to run out to his position and carry him back here before the next round hits. Do you understand?"

Jansen thought to himself that he understood that he was being asked to something extraordinarily stupid.

But rather than a snarky reply, the young private responded, "Yes sergeant," without any added comments.

Collins and Jansen took their positions standing behind the closest trees to Wilson's position and waited for the next mortar round to hit. They heard the whistle and then an explosion and immediately ran out into the field toward Lieutenant Wilson.

Just as they were reaching Wilson, Jansen heard the whistle of an incoming mortar round. Jansen looked for anything that would provide him some cover and found nothing nearby so he hit the dirt and prayed that he would not be injured by the explosion. Jansen heard the round land about five yards away from him, but the round did not explode.

"It's a dud!" Collins yelled, "Come on kid, let's grab the LT."

Collins and Jansen quickly stood up and lifted Lieutenant Wilson to his feet, slinging the young lieutenant's arms around their shoulders and sprinting back to the safety of the tree line.

Now that the last American soldier was safely behind cover, the German mortar crew ceased their attack.

Collins and Jansen carried Wilson away from the field and laid him down in the middle of one of the narrow streets.

"Where are you hit sir?" Collins asked.

"In the backside," Wilson responded somewhat sheepishly.

Collins and Jansen rolled Wilson over on his stomach. Blood was seeping into the young officer's uniform near a large tear on his butt.

"Looks like you got shot in the ass, sir," Collins blurted out, "Didn't they teach you to keep your ass down when you were in OCS?"

"How bad is it Collins?" Wilson said angrily.

"Let me take a look. Jansen help me to expose the wound," Collins said as the two men worked to open up the tear in the lieutenant's trousers so they could get a better look at the injured area.

Collins was having fun at the young officer's expense, and Jansen was trying to keep a straight face as he and Collins continued to work on Wilson's wound.

CROSSING OVER AT REMAGEN

They could see the wound better and they could see knew that it was not serious. But they still needed to cut through Wilson's underwear to properly treat his injury. Collins took out his knife and cut through the remaining layer of clothing to expose the wound.

"Don't worry sir, this doesn't look bad, whatever hit you only grazed your butt. If you had hopes of being sent home because of this injury, I don't think you are going to be that lucky. Jansen, go over to where O'Connor is helping the other men from Wilson's platoon and get a dressing and some sulfa powder."

Jansen got up and went over talk to the medic. Jansen walked up to O'Connor as the medic was working on the other soldiers that had been injured during the mortar attack.

"Hey Doc, Collins needs a field dressing and some sulfa power. Can you spare any?" Jansen asked.

O'Connor, who was cleaning out a wound on the back of a soldier's neck, replied, "My bag is over there, just take what you need. Oh, and tell Collins that I'll be over there to help him out as soon as I'm finished up with these guys. It was sheer luck that none of them were seriously hurt."

Jansen found the medic's bag, grabbed the dressing and the sulfa, and then returned to where Sergeant Collins was working on Lieutenant Wilson.

When Jansen rejoined Collins and Wilson, the platoon sergeant was doing his best to clean up the blood around the wound on Lieutenant Wilson's butt cheek.

"Hey, look at that private," Collins said to Jansen as he returned with the needed supplies, "Just as I thought, the young lieutenant here doesn't even have a single hair on his ass. In my experience being young and stupid go hand in hand. Hopefully, he will learn from this mistake."

Lieutenant Wilson had had enough and finally snapped at Collins, "Sergeant, do I need to remind you that I am your superior officer?"

"Sir," Collins said gruffly, "if you are my superior, then you need to start acting like it. You could have gotten yourself and your men killed today. Hell, if that last mortar round had exploded like it was supposed to, Jansen and I probably would have bought it trying to save your stupid ass. I suggest you just shut up and think about how lucky you were here today and thank God that your stupid decision to lead your men out into an open area in a combat zone didn't get you and your men killed."

After that, the conversation between Collins and Wilson was brief and to the point. Jansen and Collins finished cleaning and dressing Wilson's wounds. Soon O'Connor came over to evaluate the lieutenant's condition.

Only Wilson and one other soldier had to be taken to the battalion aid station. O'Connor waited with the wounded men as Jansen and Collins rejoined their platoon.

Jansen returned to his squad and took the machine gun back from Harrison.

"Good job out there Jansen, how's the LT?" Harrison asked.

"Thanks," Jansen replied as he sat down, "Wilson should be fine, Doc is sending him back to battalion aid. Collins thinks that Wilson's wound is pretty minor and that he won't be sent home."

"Well, that's great! That's just our luck. We get to keep the idiot lieutenant that nearly got half of his men killed," Harrison lamented.

"At least we don't have to worry about him for the next few days," Jansen commented.

Before long, Captain Horn shifted his men's position slightly to the west where the gap between Erpel and Unkel was not quite as wide and the open part had more cover and concealment than the open field that Lieutenant Wilson marched his men into when they had been attacked.

The men of Mike Company crossed the open area one at a time and made it to the outskirts of Unkel without taking any more enemy fire. As the company regrouped, they could more clearly see and hear the battle for the town that was already underway.

CHAPTER NINE

UNKEL

March 8, 1945
1700 Hours

Mike Company regrouped at the outskirts of Unkel, which was just an arbitrary border that separated the towns of Erpel and Unkel. The company split up into two groups and started to make their way down the narrow streets of the German village.

Jansen was feeling the effects of fatigue on his body. The thirty-one-pound Browning machine gun seemed to be getting heavier with every step. Jansen tried to focus on the task ahead and tried to forget about how tired he was as his unit began to enter the streets of Unkel.

The narrow streets meant that the men had to march single file. The column of soldiers was pretty spread out except for Jansen and Harrison. They needed to be close together because if the platoon started taking fire, the Browning machine gun was the best resource available to lay down suppressive fire. And to do that, it was important to have the man carrying the machine gun close to the man carrying the ammunition.

Mike Company came to an intersection. As soon as the first man in the column peeked around the corner the company began to take fire. The men moved back to the cover of the surrounding buildings. Sergeant Collins quickly determined where the enemy was located. The shots were coming from a building just around the corner on the opposite side of the street from where they were trying to cross.

Collins motioned for Jansen and Harrison to come up to the intersection.

"I need the Browning set up on this side of the street on the corner of that building over there." He pointed where he wanted the machine gun deployed, "Once you two get set up, I need you to lay down some suppressive fire so the rest of your squad can clear out that house."

Jansen and Harrison moved toward the intersection and stopped just short of the corner. Jansen extended the bipod legs and lifted the cover on the machine gun. Jansen was expecting Harrison to take the machine gun back because he usually did most of the shooting, but instead, Harrison just handed Jansen a belt of ammo. Jansen placed the rounds in the receiver and locked down the cover.

Jansen and Harrison slowly crawled into position. The two men found a planter box that they figured would give them some cover. It was getting close to sunset so the light was beginning to fade and there were plenty of places with dark shadows where the two soldiers could hide.

Jansen could barely see into the house. Occasionally, he could see a German soldier moving by one of the windows. Aiming really would not be an option for him, he would be forced to fire blind. Jansen decided to wait for another German to pass by a window, which would be his cue to start firing.

After a while, he saw a German helmet appear in one of the windows of the small house and opened fire. Jansen could see movement inside the house as other German soldiers dove for cover. Immediately, the rest of the squad leaped into action. Sergeant Parker led a small group across the street and approached the building hugging the buildings on the far side of the street. The first window of the house had been broken out. Parker threw a hand grenade into the house through the open window.

Jansen stopped firing so that Parker and his men could position themselves next to the door as the men waited for the grenade to explode. Jansen continued to watch the windows.

The grenade exploded. Then Parker and his team waited and listened for a few seconds before going into the house in case the Germans wanted to surrender.

Parker did not have to wait long. As the Americans waited outside, the door of the house slowly opened and a hand waving a white handkerchief emerged from inside the house. They moved into a better position and trained their M1 Garand rifles on the door. Soon the door opened fully, and four German soldiers exited the building with their hands on the air yelling, "Nicht schießen!" By now every soldier in Jansen's unit knew enough German to understand that the Germans were saying, "Don't shoot!"

Parker and his men relieved the Germans of their weapons and walked the prisoners back to where the rest of the platoon was located. All of the POWs were able to walk, but two of the Germans were wounded.

One of the Germans was missing his helmet and was bleeding from his scalp. Jansen figured that this was the soldier he was aiming at when he started firing and that he had hit the German in the helmet. The bullet must have grazed the soldier's head. The other wounded prisoner was limping, it looked to Jansen like the man had been hit in the leg by shrapnel from Parker's grenade.

Sergeant Collins sent four soldiers from another squad to go in and clear the house to make sure that there were not any other German soldiers hiding inside. After a few minutes, the soldiers emerged from the house and declared that it was "Kraut free."

Collins then chose four "volunteers" to escort the prisoners to the rear.

With the intersection cleared, the company continued its push north into the heart of Unkel. The company had safely made it across the intersection and were carefully making their way down the next section of the street. Jansen was still carrying the machine gun and Harrison was staying close to his teammate.

"Jansen, you did well back there, laying down the suppressive fire."

"Thanks, Harrison, just let me know when you want to carry the Browning again."

"Well, I don't want to carry that thing, but I'll take it the next time I get an itchy trigger finger," Harrison joked.

The company continued its advance northward. After advancing several blocks without incident, the column stopped. Jansen could see Collins go to the front of the column. The men at the head of the company were slowly and quietly getting down and taking cover.

Soon Sergeant Collins returned and went over to where Jansen and Harrison were waiting, "The lead squad spotted a barrier across the street about 500 yards north of their position. It is hard to tell, but it looks like the Nazis have moved in some dirt and created a defensive position. I want you two to go up and join the other machine gun team that is already up there. I don't know if the Germans know that we are approaching their position yet or not. So, I think if we are careful, we should be able to get a little closer before we start drawing fire. When that happens, I want you and the other machine gun team to find the best position you can and give the rest of the company enough cover fire so that they can advance. You understand?"

The two soldiers nodded, "No questions, Sarge," Harrison responded.

Jansen and Harrison slowly began advancing toward the front of the column taking care to stay low and use whatever concealment was available.

Soon the two had reached the front of the column. A sergeant motioned for Jansen and Harrison to position themselves on the far side of the street opposite from the other machine gun crew.

The company advanced down the street slowly and deliberately, doing whatever they could to stay quiet and hidden. The company was able to move north without taking fire, either because they were unnoticed, or because the Germans were waiting for the Americans to get closer to their position before they opened fire.

As they would pass by the windows of a house, the men leading the column of soldiers would look in the windows of the house to check to see if there was any evidence that Germans were occupying it. If there was any question, a couple of men would clear the house before moving on. The last thing the men of Mike Company needed was to walk into an ambush.

The streets of Unkel were narrow, but the fronts of the buildings were not built to be flush with the neighboring building, so there were plenty of nooks and crannies where the soldiers could hide as they approached the German's defensive position.

Soon they were close enough to their objective that Jansen could see movement behind the berm. It was not clear that the Germans knew that the Americans were approaching. It could be that they were waiting to draw the Allied troops in closer before they opened fire.

A platoon leader close to the front of the column noticed this as well and motioned for the men to get down and take cover. The lead part of the column was now only about 200 yards away from the German position.

Jansen and Harrison looked for a position where they could set up their machine gun because they figured that the Germans were about to open fire. They found a small open area between two houses that would work, but it was still about five yards north of their position. A shot rang out. A man on the opposite side of the street from them went down grabbing his thigh as the blood from a bullet wound ran down his leg.

Jansen and Harrison crawled to the position they had spotted earlier. Jansen unfolded the bipod on the front of the machine gun and started firing at the enemy position.

At this range, it was not hard to find specific targets. Jansen knew that his job was to make it as difficult for the Germans to fire on the advancing men from his company.

The men of Mike Company continued to advance past Jansen's position. Soon a soldier at the front of the column was close enough to the German position to throw a hand grenade over the berm of dirt and into the German's position. After the grenade exploded the Americans rushed toward the German position, trying to close in on them as quickly as possible.

Jansen kept firing on the German soldiers as more and more GI's converged on their position. Soon the Germans began waving a white flag and the skirmish was over.

As the sun began to set, the Americans took about twenty German prisoners and escorted them to the rear to join the rest of the POWs.

Captain Horn joined the men at the berm they had just captured and told the men to set up a defensive perimeter so that they could take a break and eat dinner.

The company's defensive line was only about a hundred yards long. As such, this allowed the men of Mike Company to have only a few people on the line, while the rest of them could get a chance to eat.

Jansen and Harrison moved forward to the line that the German's previously held. Soon the rest of their squad joined them. Collins assigned their squad to occupy a small home on the front line.

There was no evidence that the Germans were planning a counterattack. It could be that the twenty Germans the company captured was the entire force protecting this section of the German line.

Jansen followed the rest of his squad to the house that Collins had ordered them to protect. Parker knocked on the front door, after he was convinced that the house was empty, Parker and the rest of the squad entered. They quickly checked to make sure that the house was indeed unoccupied and then Parker assigned two men to guard the windows of the house that faced the street.

Jansen and Harrison sat down together, took off their web gear, and pulled their K-rations out of their combat packs. The men then began the process of opening the small cans of food and started to eat.

Between bites, Jansen turned to Harrison and asked, "Do you feel like taking the Browning for a while after this?"

"Sure, I'll take it off your hands for you," said Harrison.

The house was small, so there was not much room for the men to spread out. Soon Ellison came over and sat down with Jansen and Harrison.

"Is it okay if I join you?" Ellison asked.

"Not at all, have a seat," Harrison answered. Jansen was surprised, he had never seen Harrison talk to a Replacement before if he did not have to. Harrison continued, "Good job out there today Ellison, you somehow managed to stay alive."

"Thanks, Harrison," came the reply.

"I thought life on a farm during the Depression was hard," Jansen interjected between bites of food, "but I have never been more tired in my life."

"Yeah, I know," said Ellison, "what time did we get up this morning? 0330 hours? I can tell you; I don't care where I am when all this is over, I am going to sleep like a baby."

"It's best if you don't think about rest, it will only make you feel more tired," Harrison explained, "I have a feeling that they are going to be pushing us hard for quite a while. Also, I guess that the farther we push north, the harder the Germans will be fighting back."

"You're probably right," Jansen replied and looked down at his last box of K-rations that was now empty. Then something occurred to him, "Hey, Harrison, if they are only moving troops over the bridge, how are we going to get food? Because this is all the food we have left."

"Good question, I don't rightly know," he replied, "I suppose we will have to scrounge for food."

Jansen looked out a nearby window and could see the shadows getting longer in the streets of Unkel. A warm gold light fell on the buildings and surrounding hills as he finished his meal.

Soon Collins stopped by and told the men that they had to pack up and get back out onto the streets. One of the other companies from their battalion had leapfrogged over their position and the regiment had made it to the northern edge of the town. The Americans had just captured the German town of Unkel.

CHAPTER TEN

SCHEUREN

March 8, 1945
1830 Hours

The sun had just set, it was now 1830 hours. Jansen had finished up his K-rations, not knowing exactly how he would get his next meal. Harrison grabbed the machine gun and Jansen slung the ammo satchels over his shoulders. After the two engagements with the Germans, the ammo satchels were getting a bit lighter.

Jansen walked out of the house they were occupying and onto the streets of Unkel. It was getting darker now and the air was getting colder. There were American troops everywhere. Most were from his division, the 78th, but he also noticed groups of soldiers from some other unit because they were not wearing the 78th Lightning Division unit patch on their shoulders.

There were groups of captured German soldiers being escorted to the rear. Collins called his platoon together.

"As you can see, the front line has moved north. Captain Horn wants us to move out and relieve Kilo Company on the front line. Since other elements of the 311th have already swept through here, we shouldn't have to worry too much about taking enemy fire until we get to the edge of Scheuren. But I still want you to be smart as we advance up to the front lines. Remember what happened to Lieutenant Wilson and his men? I don't want us to make the same mistake again."

It only took the men a few minutes to move through Unkel and make it to the front lines of the battle. They met up with some men from another company in their battalion. Jansen noticed that Captain Horn had come forward in his jeep and linked up with the other company commander. Before long, a plan was passed down to Jansen's squad. Sergeant Parker called his men together.

"There is a squad of Germans occupying a house about 200 yards from here. We have a squad from Kilo Company in that house over there." Parker pointed towards a small two-story house nestled in amongst some trees, "we will advance on the German position and the squad from Kilo Company will provide cover fire for us. Harrison and Jansen, you will cover the exits on this side of the house. We won't worry too much about any Nazis that want to retreat, we just don't want to be forced to track down and flush out any Germans behind our lines. The rest of the squad will go in and clear the house."

After a few questions, the squad was ready to move out. As they approached the house occupied by the men from Kilo Company, Parker slowly moved over to one of the doors to the house, knocked, and said, "3rd of the 311th."

The door opened and a soldier from Kilo Company told Parker that his squad was clear to advance on the enemy-held house.

Luckily, there were plenty of trees and vegetation that the men could use for concealment as they approached their objective. Additionally, it had been over half an hour since the sun had set, the fading light made it easier for the men to move undetected.

Jansen was carrying his M1 Carbine and was staying next to Harrison as the squad moved forward. They were about one hundred yards from the house when they started taking fire. Immediately the men for Kilo Company started firing on the German-occupied house.

Parker's squad continued to advance on the house. They were now only about fifty yards out, but there was no cover or concealment that the men could use to cover the last fifty yards.

Parker motioned for Jansen and Harrison to set up the machine gun behind a short rock wall to their right.

Jansen followed Harrison and the two men got into position and set up the machine gun and waited for the signal. Parker got the rest of his men into position to rush the house. Parker signaled to Harrison to begin firing. Harrison squeezed the trigger on the Browning and began spraying bullets into the lower floor of the house. The Germans inside the house dove for cover and the rest of the squad rushed toward the house.

One of Germans on the second floor started firing on Parker's men while the rest continued to exchange fire with the men from Kilo Company in the other house. One of Parker's men, Corporal Rogers, was hit in the shoulder. Rogers continued to advance toward the house with his squad. A combination of adrenalin and self-preservation helped to drive him forward. If he fell now, he would be out in the open and an easy target for the Germans.

Jansen could see the German soldier that shot Rogers, the German soldier was partially leaning out of one of the second-floor windows so that he could get a better aim on the Americans approaching below him. Jansen fired three shots with his carbine and the German soldier screamed something in German and then his lifeless body slumped over the windowsill.

The men rushing toward the house threw grenades into the ground floor windows, Harrison redirected his fire to the second-story windows. Jansen could see his squad rush into the house. The injured Rogers made it to the outside wall of the house and sat down with his back leaning up against the foundation.

Jansen could see a flash from a grenade exploding in one of the upstairs rooms. Harrison knew that was his cue to stop firing. Harrison aimed the machine gun on the door of the house in case any of the Germans tried to escape. The gunfire stopped and before long the squad emerged with six German prisoners. The Germans had their hands on their heads and walked into the area between Jansen and Harrison's position and the house.

Jansen and Harrison got up from their position and joined the rest of their squad. Parker yelled, "Get on your knees!" to the

German prisoners. The German's just stood there; it was clear that they did not understand what Parker was telling them to do.

Parker grabbed one of the German prisoners by the shoulder and pushed him forward forcing the man to his knees, "I said, 'on your knees,' you Nazi bastard!" Parker yelled. The rest of the Germans finally understood what was expected of them and dropped to their knees as well.

Meanwhile, two men went over to see how Corporal Rogers was doing and began addressing his injury.

"We are going to have to take these Krauts back to Captain Horn," Parker said, "Monroe, I want you, Jansen, and Ellison to walk them back."

"Sure thing, Parker," Monroe replied.

Parker yelled over to the injured soldier, "Hey, Rogers! How bad is it?"

"The bullet grazed my shoulder and missed the bone," the corporal replied.

"Can you walk?" Parker asked.

His fellow soldiers had already applied a field dressing to his shoulder and helped Rogers to his feet, "Yeah, I should be okay."

"Great, go with the prisoners back to the rear, and make sure these two Replacements don't do anything stupid," Parker said looking at Jansen and Ellison.

Jansen figured that is why Parker added Monroe to their group. Deep down, he still did not trust any of the new soldiers in his unit.

"Jansen, before you leave give the ammo belts to Harrison, I think he is going to need them," said Parker.

The two machine gunners had already used up quite a bit of ammunition. Jansen consolidated the belts into one of the satchels.

"Here you go Harrison, I'll keep the empty satchel and see if I scrounge up some more ammo belts on our way back," Jansen said as he handed the satchel full of ammo to Harrison.

"Thanks, Jansen."

The four Americans headed toward the rear while the rest of the squad reentered the house they had just taken. Parker's squad then waited for the men from Kilo Company to advance to their position. The lines were pretty fluid at this point in the battle and dealing with

German prisoners was the main thing slowing down the American's advance.

The German prisoners walked with their hands on their heads. Jansen and the other two soldiers always had their rifles pointed at the backs of the prisoners.

The rush of adrenalin that comes from being in combat wore off and Jansen's body immediately reminded him that he had been up and moving since three-thirty that morning. A wave of fatigue washed over his body as they marched through the dark streets of Scheuren, Germany.

As they walked through the German town and as the group of Americans and their prisoners were farther away from the fighting Jansen noticed that the German prisoners began to talk. Jansen almost expected one of the Veterans to order the Germans to shut up, but neither of them said a word. Probably because Corporal Rogers was injured and had more serious matters on his mind and as for Private Monroe, it seemed he was more worried about being in charge of Jansen and Ellison to notice something as minor as the German prisoners having a quiet conversation.

Jansen decided to do his best to listen in on what the prisoners were saying as they marched along. The Germans were talking about how surprised they were that the Americans were able to push the German forces north so quickly. Then the Germans mentioned something important. They began talking about a group of reinforcements that were expected to arrive to help stop the American advance. Jansen began listening intently to what was said next. One of the prisoners said that the 600 reinforcements would arrive at the battle soon. Jansen just pretended he did not hear anything and just marched through the dark streets with the information he had just obtained.

Soon the men found Horn's jeep parked in front of a small German cottage. They could see people from their company coming out of the home as they approached.

Monroe turned to Rogers, "Corporal, go in there and let Captain Horn know that we are outside with six prisoners."

"Roger that, Monroe," Rogers replied and then walked over to the house and went inside.

A couple of minutes later Horn came out to talk to his men, "Rogers is inside getting looked at by one of the medics. I want to interrogate one of the prisoners here before we send them all back to the rear. Battalion has a collection point for POWs down in Erpel."

Horn looked over the prisoners, "This Kraut right here is a sergeant, let's take him inside and question him before sending the six of them back to Erpel. Jansen, can you help me ask this POW some questions?"

"Yes, sir, I'll do my best," Jansen replied.

"Good, bring that prisoner into the house so that we can have a little chat," said Horn.

Jansen told the German prisoner to follow Captain Horn and the three entered the small house. There was wood burning in the fireplace and Jansen immediately noticed how much warmer it was inside. Horn motioned for the German soldier to sit down at a small table that was in the center of the room. Horn sat across from the German and Jansen stood there with his rifle trained on the POW.

Jansen turned to Horn and said, "Sir, I have something I would like to say before we start."

"What is it private?"

"Sir," Jansen began, "while marching these prisoners over here I overheard them talk about a force of 600 German reinforcements that they are expecting to arrive soon."

"Good job Jansen, we can definitely use that. Start by asking for his name," Horn told Jansen.

Jansen asked the question. The German was visibly stunned that Jansen was speaking to him in German, even if it was rather broken. The prisoner replied, "Hans Schneider."

Horn turned to Jansen, "Now ask him about the reinforcements, we need to know when they are supposed to arrive."

Jansen told the German that he knew about the reinforcements and wanted to know what time they were expected. The German indicated that he did not know and then added that with the extra troops the Germans were sending they were going to retake the Ludendorff Bridge.

Jansen turned to Horn and said, "Sir, he claims he doesn't know when the new troops will arrive. But he did say that the Germans are planning a counterattack to retake the bridge."

"Good work, Jansen," Horn said, "That means that he is admitting that what you heard was right, the reinforcements are coming." The captain then grabbed the field phone that was on the table and relayed that information back to battalion headquarters.

Horn told Jansen that Rogers would stay in the house until a truck or jeep could give him a ride to the aid station in Erpel. And that they needed to march the prisoners back to the holding area and then get back to Scheuren as soon as possible so that they could rejoin their squad. Jansen thought to himself that Horn must have known that his unit would be needed for something that was planned for later that night.

After that, Jansen escorted the prisoner back outside and rejoined his group. Walking out into the cold air was quite a shock after spending time in the warm little house. It was getting later and by now it was completely dark. The men could hear that the battle was still moving farther north and away from their position.

"The old man wants us to march these prisoners back to Erpel and then we have to high tail it back to the front line," Jansen explained, "I think headquarters has something big planned for later on tonight."

"We'd better get going then," said Monroe as he pushed the German soldier that had just been questioned back in the small formation with the other POWs.

The three Americans walked through the dark streets back to the outskirts of Erpel. They had to ask around but eventually found the POW collection point. There were plenty of groups of POWs being turned in. After they had handed the prisoners off to the MPs Jansen noticed a couple of soldiers with a circular unit patch that he did not recognize. Curiosity got the better of him.

"Hey Monroe," Jansen asked, "What unit are those guys with?"

"I have no idea," Monroe answered dismissively.

Ellison decided on his own that he was going to find the answer to Jansen's question and approached the soldiers, "Hey, you're not with the 78th, what unit are you with?"

"We're with the 9th ID, we have been trying to push east, but it hasn't been easy, the Germans have the high ground there."

"Yeah, we have been pushing north since we crossed the bridge earlier today," said Ellison, "Good luck, and keep your head down."

Ellison turned to Jansen, "There you go, there were from the 9th Infantry Division. Does satisfy your curiosity?"

"Yeah," Jansen replied, "I suppose we'd better get back. Also, if you see an armorer let me know, I told Harrison I would try to find some more ammo belts on our way back."

The three men began heading north. They were in the town of Unkel when Ellison spotted a supply truck with a supply sergeant standing behind it. Jansen could see that the truck was loaded with ammo crates. He walked over to the back of the truck, "Hello sarge, do you have any .30-06 ammo belts?"

"What unit you with soldier?"

"3rd Battalion, 311th Infantry Regiment," Jansen replied.

"I'm with 2nd Battalion, so I can only give you a couple of belts. If you need more, you will have to get it from your unit."

The supply sergeant pulled one of the crates out of the back of the truck, opened it up, and handed Jansen the ammo.

"Thanks, sarge, this should be enough," Jansen replied as he stuffed the belts into his satchel.

Munroe looked at Jansen, "Can we head back now?" he said impatiently.

It was now completely dark, there was still a steady stream of traffic taking soldiers north to the front lines. Luckily all the traffic was headed away from them so the three men did not have to worry about being blinded in the night by the headlights of oncoming vehicles.

The three men marched into the night. It was now after 2000 hours and the air was getting colder as Jansen and his fellow soldiers marched north. Jansen wondered how hard it would be to link back up with his unit once they made it back to Scheuren considering how quickly the Americans had been advancing into German-held territory.

The men passed through the streets of Unkel. Once they arrived in Scheuren, they decided to see if Captain Horn was still using the same house for the company headquarters. They arrived at the small home and found it empty.

"What do we do now?" Ellison asked.

"We continue north and look for any American unit we can find," Monroe said.

Jansen could tell that the fighting had died down and he worried that finding the front lines would be hard in the dark. He was concerned that they could accidentally stumble into an area too close to the German lines and get shot.

"I think we should try to make it back to the house where we took the German prisoners," Jansen said, "At least we know that the front line has to be somewhere north of that house."

The three men continued down the dark streets, constantly looking for any evidence of an American unit. They continued north for a few blocks when Monroe suddenly stopped.

"Look, over there," he said pointing down one of the side streets.

There, in the darkness was an American jeep parked in front of one of the German houses.

"Let's see if anyone is inside," Monroe said as he began walking toward the building.

As they approached the home Jansen could see light coming from inside, which he saw as a good sign. As they got closer, they could see a soldier standing guard by the front door. As the three men walked up to the guard Monroe asked, "Are you with the 311th?"

"Yes, what do you want?" the guard asked.

"We are from Third Battalion and we are trying to find Mike Company," Monroe answered.

"This is Second Battalion," the guard answered, "Third Battalion was moved to cover the line east of here, near the river."

"Do you have a field phone we can use? So we can call our CO and let him know we are coming?" Monroe asked.

The guard yelled into the house, "Hey Chandler, some guys from Third Battalion want to use the field phone, is it okay to send them in?"

Jansen could hear a voice from inside the house say, "Yeah, that's okay. Send them in."

The guard stepped aside, and the three men entered the house. Inside it was warm and dimly lit. Over in a corner of the house was a field phone setting on a table. There was a private sitting at the table. He grabbed the phone and cranked the handle, "I'll ring up the switchboard, who are you trying to call?" he asked.

Ellison answered, "Mike Company, Third Battalion."

Monroe looked at Ellison to let him know that Monroe should be the one talking.

"Okay got it," the private answered and then began talking into the handset, "Battalion switchboard? Can you connect me to Third Battalion? Yeah, I'm trying to reach Mike Company."

He then turned to Monroe, "They are going to connect me." There was a short pause, "Hello, Mike Company? Yeah, hold on, I have some of your men here who want to talk."

"Here you go," the private said as he handed the handset to Monroe.

"Hello, this is Private Monroe, we need directions to your position," Monroe said.

There was another short pause. Then Monroe said, "Okay, got it," and then handed the phone back to the soldier who had helped them make the call.

"Thanks for your help," Monroe said.

Monroe turned to Jansen and Ellison, "The Company is basically due east of here, they are right next to the Rhine River. If head east we should find them, no problem."

Jansen, Ellison, and Monroe left the house and headed east toward the river. As they got closer to the river there were no more houses nor streets and the three found themselves passing through a wooded area.

Before long they came to a road than ran north to south. One by one the men rushed across the open area and made it to the other side of the road safely.

Soon they approached the river, but the soldiers did not see any evidence of Mike Company. Monroe decided that they should turn north and follow the river. The night had gotten eerily quiet. Jansen guessed that the Americans and the Germans sides must have both dug in for the night. The cold night air was becoming more noticeable and Jansen dreaded the idea of jumping into a foxhole and standing watch as the cold from the winter night slowly penetrated his body.

Monroe spoke to the two Replacements in a low voice, "Keep your eyes open. As quiet as it is right now, it would be really easy to accidentally get too close to the front lines and end up getting picked off by the Germans."

The men began to move slowly and carefully northward through the night. After a few minutes of walking, Jansen could see a faint light up ahead. The three soldiers made their way toward the light trying to stay hidden in the shadows. As they got closer, they could make out the outline of a jeep.

Soon they could see Captain Horn holding a flashlight and standing next to the jeep looking over a map that was spread out on the hood.

"Americans," Monroe called out as the three approached their CO.

Horn looked up, "Glad you were able to find us. The rest of the company is dug in for now, but I think command has something planned for us later tonight. Are you three all from the same squad?"

"Yes sir. Sergeant Parker is our squad leader," Monroe answered.

"Parker is in Sergeant Collins' platoon. You see those three trees over there?" Horn asked Monroe.

"Yes sir."

"Collins is just on the other side of those trees. He can tell you where your squad is. But make sure you stay low and quiet, there aren't many Germans in this area, but I am sure that they would be happy to take out an American who was just walking around and making himself a target," Horn told the men.

"Thank you, sir," Monroe said. Then the men made their way over to Sergeant Collins' position.

"Hello sarge, we are back," Monroe whispered to Collins as the three approached his position.

Collins squinted trying to recognize the face of the men approaching him, "Is that you Monroe?"

"Yes, sarge, and I have Jansen and Ellison with me. We just got back from escorting some German prisoners down to Erpel."

Collins informed the men that they had dug in as best they could, but that they were told that they would be moving out later that night. Collins took the three men to Sergeant Parker.

Collins and Parker agreed that Parker would take Ellison and Monroe to their positions and that Collins would take Jansen over to where Harrison was positioned on the line.

The night was eerily quiet, although Jansen could hear gunfire east of their position as the two men approached Harrison. He was behind a tree next to a narrow dirt road that cut through the heavily wooded forest.

"Harrison is right over there private," Collins said pointing to the tree where Harrison was located.

"Thanks, sarge," Jansen replied and then began to carefully make his way to Harrison.

"Hello Harrison," Jansen said as he approached the position.

"It's about time, what took you so long?" Jansen could tell that his absence had annoyed Harrison.

"We had to march the prisoners all the way back to Erpel. But I was able to get us some extra ammo for the Browning," Jansen said as he put the satchel full of ammo belts on the ground next to the machine gun.

"Well, that's good news. I think we are going to need it before we are done," said Harrison, "It's been pretty quiet, so I didn't use much ammo while you were gone. Why don't you take over manning the machine gun?"

"Will do," Jansen said as the two traded places. Jansen settled in and raised the stock of the M1919 to his shoulder. Jansen looked through the sights of the machine gun and began to visually scan the area. He could see nothing that would indicate that there were any enemy positions near him.

"Are there any Germans out there that I should know about?" Jansen asked.

"I didn't see anything, but we didn't get here until after it was already pretty dark. If there are Germans out there, they are keeping themselves well hidden," Harrison replied.

There was a small mound of dirt that the men were positioned behind. Jansen and Harrison were lying spread eagle on the ground.

Luckily, Harrison had found a patch of earth that was fairly dry. As he laid on the ground, Jansen could feel that he was losing body heat as the cold from the night air and ground penetrated his body.

The events of the day began to replay in Jansen's mind as he tried to fight off the fatigue and the cold. Jansen settled into his job.

CHAPTER ELEVEN

THE MARCH

March 8, 1945
2100 Hours

Jansen and Harrison traded off manning the machine gun every half hour or so. Jansen had neither seen nor heard anything that would indicate there were German troops near their position.

If it were not for the cold, it would have been almost impossible for Jansen and Harrison to stay awake. Even though Jansen was awoken less than 24 hours ago at 0330 hours, that event seemed like a lifetime ago. When they were not manning the machine gun, Jansen and Harrison fought fatigue and the urge to sleep.

As the night progressed the temperature continued to drop. The two soldiers stayed at their post monitoring an area that both were beginning to believe was not occupied by any German forces.

Jansen and Harrison had spent hours fighting the cold, fatigue, and boredom. It was now almost midnight. Jansen had just taken over manning the Browning when Harrison suddenly sat up.

"Do you hear that?" Harrison asked.

Jansen listened carefully. Off in the distance, he could hear the rumble of an engine.

"Yeah, what do you think it is?" Jansen replied.

"It kind of sounds like a truck and I think it's coming down this road," Harrison said.

Before long Jansen could see the lights of the truck illuminating the trees that lined the narrow gravel road.

"Harrison, what do I do?" Jansen asked excitedly.

"Wait until it gets a little closer, then open up and aim for the tires and the engine. If the truck doesn't stop, then aim for the driver," Harrison answered.

Soon the truck came into view as it approached Jansen's position. He waited until the truck was about 100 yards away, aimed at the truck's front tires, and then squeezed the trigger on the machine gun. When Jansen saw that one of the front tires had been hit, he shifted his aim to the vehicle's engine. Jansen could see either smoke or steam coming out from under the vehicle's hood, so he adjusted his aim once again and began firing at the back tires. Jansen was about to take aim at the cab of the truck when he noticed that it had begun to slow down. The truck eventually drove off the road and stopped about fifteen yards away from their position. Two German soldiers emerged from the cab of the truck with their hands in the air.

Sergeant Parker was close by and had seen everything that had just happened.

He yelled over to Jansen, "Jansen, tell those damn Krauts to drop their weapons and walk forward to your position and then turn around. I'll come over and help you with the prisoners."

Jansen yelled at the two soldiers in German and told them to drop their weapons and walk forward. The Germans took their pistols out of their holsters and laid them on the ground and walked along the shoulder of the road toward Jansen and Harrison. When the Germans reached the tree next to Jansen's position, Jansen told them to stop and turn around and to put their hands on their heads.

By this time, Parker had made it over there, "Jansen, keep up the good work and you may accidentally turn into a real soldier."

"Thanks, sarge," Jansen replied

"I'll take these two back to see the captain. Meanwhile, you two check out that truck and make sure that there aren't any more Krauts hiding in the back."

Parker grabbed another man from his squad and marched the two German prisoners back to Captain Horn's jeep.

After all that excitement Jansen and Harrison were even more convinced that there were not any Germans in the immediate area. Even so, they stayed behind the tree line for cover as they approached the truck. In the dark, it was hard to see, but there did not appear to be anyone near the truck as they approached it from the side. The two crept around to the back of the truck. There was no room for anyone to hide in the back of the truck because it was packed to the hilt with crates.

"Jansen, can you make out what is printed on these crates?"

Jansen took out his flashlight and examined the writing on the crates and said, "I think it says that these crates are carrying explosives!"

"Good God! What do you think was their plan?" Harrison said while slowly backing away.

"I don't know. Maybe the Krauts were going to try again to blow up the bridge?" Jansen answered.

"We can't just leave it here. You stay here and guard the truck and I will go tell Sergeant Collins what we found," Harrison told Jansen, "If I see anyone, I will send them over to help you."

With that, Harrison was off, and Jansen suddenly found himself alone in the woods, ahead of the American lines, in the middle of the night, guarding a truck full of dangerous explosives. Jansen crawled under the rear axle of the German truck and aimed the Browning to the north. He figured that if any German soldiers would stumble upon his position, they would be coming from that direction. It was a good place to hide and that position gave him a good view of the road and a large section of the woods.

Jansen hunkered down and waited. It was eerily quiet in the woods as Jansen waited for what seemed to be an eternity.

Before long, Jansen heard a familiar voice, "Jansen, where are you?" The voice belonged to Ellison who was approaching his position from behind.

"I'm underneath the truck," Jansen answered as he made his way out from his position to meet his friend. Ellison had two other soldiers with him.

"Boy, am I glad to see you," Jansen said as he climbed to his feet.

"We are here to rescue you," Ellison said lightheartedly, "Collins wants us to set up a perimeter around the truck and wait for Harrison to get back from battalion HQ."

Jansen was happy that he was no longer alone. The situation of being alone in the woods was beginning to bother him. Even if he would be required to stay where he was, it was nice that he was no longer alone.

The four men each took a position at a different corner of the truck and set up a small perimeter around the vehicle. Jansen and Ellison set up at the rear of the truck. Soon Jansen learned from his friend that Collins had sent Harrison to battalion headquarters to get a deuce-and-a-half and guide it back to this position so that they could offload the explosives and take them to the rear, well behind the American lines.

In the meantime, Collins decided to advance their platoon's position farther north so that it was even with the captured German truck. Collins did this because, even though he was generally extremely cautious, it was clear that the Germans were not defending this section of the line and were probably several yards from their position. So, moving the platoon forward fifteen yards was not a huge gamble.

It took about an hour for all the different parts of the plan to be completed. When the German truck was unloaded, and the line moved forward it was well after midnight. Once his platoon had settled into their new defensive positions, Collins made his way to every outpost on the line to fill them in on what was going on.

Collins told his men that Captain Horn was called to regimental headquarters to receive orders for the attack on Bad Honnef. The advance of the regiment had been halted because the command of the 311th had been passed over to the 9th Infantry Division, and this was causing some confusion as the new command structure was trying to figure out what to do. Collins asked his men to sit tight, stay awake, and be ready to move out at a moment's notice.

Harrison eventually returned from battalion HQ and rejoined Jansen and the rest of his squad. Now Jansen and Harrison were again lying on the cold ground protecting the American line from a German force that probably was not there. Jansen thought that he would prefer fighting off a German counterattack, to waiting for an attack that probably was not going to happen. His body was tired, cold, and now he was also beginning to get hungry. And since the men had already eaten their last box of K-rations, Jansen did not know when or from where he would get his next meal.

When you are bored it is hard to ignore your circumstances if you are miserable. Jansen tried not to think too much about his situation. Harrison was now manning the machine gun and Jansen was just waiting to assist Harrison in case the Germans decided to mount a counterattack.

Harrison had decided to man the machine gun after Jansen was able to, "Have all the fun," of shooting at and stopping the German truck. They had been switching off with the Browning every half hour before they encountered the truck. But now, after almost an hour, Harrison was not asking Jansen to switch with him.

At 0200 hours Horn gave orders to thin out the line. He wanted every other post to move off the line and meet near his command jeep in a clearing about 200 yards to the rear of the company's defensive positions.

Parker came over to where Jansen and Harrison were positioned and told them Horn's instructions for the company briefing.

As Jansen and Harrison were making their way to the assembly area Jansen asked Harrison, "What do you think is going on?"

"I have no idea; we should be pushing north right now. Not sitting on our asses. I'm sure Horn will let us know what the plan is soon enough," Harrison replied.

The two men walked through the night until they found the clearing where Captain Horn's jeep was located.

Some other men from the company were already there. Captain Horn was waiting until all his squad leaders had reported in before he addressed the men. Before long, half of the company was in the assembly area and Horn was ready.

"The regiment will be attacking the German lines at 0300 hours. The attack will use both first and second battalions. Since our area is not very heavily guarded by the Germans, the plan is for the Third Battalion to pass through this sector in a single file column and attack the German's right flank when the rest of the regiment's attack reaches Bad Honnef. Because this sector is still held by the Germans, we could easily find ourselves close to German soldiers on this march, so noise and light discipline will be particularly important. There will be absolutely no talking and no smoking. I will send you men back to your positions and we will wait for the rest of the battalion to arrive then we will move out. In the meantime, you will stay at your posts until the battalion has made it past our line, and then Mike Company will fall in at the end of the column."

After a few routine questions from the men, the soldiers returned to their posts, the second half of the company formed up in the assembly area, and they received the same briefing from Captain Horn.

It would take another hour after the men of Mike Company were back in their fighting positions for the rest of the companies of Third Battalion to get into position.

Just after 0300 hours, Jansen heard to the east of his position the attack by the First and Second Battalions. Shortly after that, he saw the first few men of the column of Third Battalion soldiers pass by, just west of his position.

To Jansen, it seemed to take forever before it was Mike Company's turn to move out and take its place at the end of the column.

Sergeant Parker came over to where Jansen and Harrison were manning the machine gun.

"Okay, come with me. We need to get into position. Any German troops that may have been left in the area have moved east to join the main part of the battle," Parker said in a hushed tone, "But this will be the last time anyone will be able to talk until we are in position and begin to attack the German Army's flank."

Jansen got up and picked up the satchels of ammo and moved back to the assembly area where the other men of Mike Company were already beginning to join that column and march silently into the night.

Jansen was starting to get nervous. He reached for a cigarette, which was his habit when he was getting ready to go into combat. Harrison was standing next to him, without saying a word Harrison looked at Jansen and shook his head. Jansen suddenly remembered that they were not allowed to smoke and put his pack of cigarettes back in his pocket.

Jansen thought about taking out the Bible that Chaplain Martin had given him. It did not take long for Jansen to abandon that idea as well. First off, he would not be able to read it in the middle of the night in the German woods without any light, and secondly, if Parker caught him reading the Bible Jansen would catch the wrath of his squad leader, and that was the last thing he needed right now.

Jansen decided that there was nothing to do but to say a short prayer and wait for his turn to move out.

The night was getting colder and Jansen was glad that he was not lying on the ground anymore. One by one the men of Mike Company were joining the column as the company began their march to Bad Honnef.

It was almost 0400 hours when Jansen and Harrison began the march north. The column was just a little east of the road that Jansen and Harrison had been guarding when they stopped the German truck loaded with explosives. It was important for the soldiers to have a point of reference to guide them through the German woods in the dark. The trail was far enough from the road that the trees helped to conceal the soldiers but close enough to the road so the soldiers could see it as they marched north in the night.

By this time, the trail that the battalion had taken was well worn and easy to follow. Jansen watched where he stepped, being careful not to make any noise as he marched. He was trying to move through the woods as quietly as possible. Harrison was still carrying the Browning machine gun. Jansen was grateful that he was not carrying that large weapon through the heavily wooded area.

Jansen could hear the rest of the regiment fighting to advance on the German positions to the northeast. That attack was an essential element of the plan for the Third Battalion to slip through the German lines unnoticed.

As the men marched through the woods, Jansen realized that it had now been over 24 hours since he had last slept. Jansen was not sleepy, but unbelievably tired. The march kept his mind occupied enough to ward off his body's desire for sleep. And Jansen appreciated the fact that the march was also helping him to stay warm in the cold night air.

The men were making slow progress as they marched north. The reason for this was that the men at the front of the column were slowly and quietly picking their way through the German-held territory to avoid detection. They were doing their best to get to their objective to the south of Bad Honnef unnoticed. The Third Battalion also did not want to get too far in front of the fighting. If that happened, they could easily be cut off from the rest of the regiment.

All these factors combined accounted for the slow pace of the Third Battalion's march north.

Jansen had been marching for over an hour. It was still the dead of night, but he could see that the column was beginning to break up a short distance in front of him. They had reached the outskirts of Bad Honnef.

The men were still behind the tree line as Jansen and Harrison approached the end of the march. Sergeant Collins was already a few yards back from the perimeter that was being formed at the edge of Bad Honnef and quietly directed them to their place on the newly formed line, right under the noses of the unsuspecting German forces.

From their location, they could see some of the houses in Bad Honnef through the trees. Jansen could hear that the fighting was close and getting closer. It was now a little after 0400 hours. The battle for Bad Honnef was about to begin.

CHAPTER TWELVE

BAD HONNEF

March 9, 1945
0412 Hours

Jansen and Harrison found a hollow place in the ground to set up the machine gun. They had a good view of Bad Honnef but could not see neither the American nor the German forces. They could hear that the battle was getting closer to their position as the Americans pushed the Germans north through the wooded area between Scheuren and Bad Honnef.

Jansen could not see much activity in the houses of Bad Honnef. This was a good sign, this meant that the Germans who were occupying Bad Honnef were unaware that an entire battalion was in position to attack their flank once the battle lines approached the outskirts of the city.

The Third Battalion's position stretched from where Mike Company was located almost to the Rhine. Now all the men had to do was wait for the First and Second Battalions to push the German Army into the trap they had set.

Within an hour Jansen could hear that the fighting was closing in on their position. Jansen and Harrison continued to wait at their post several yards back from the edge of the tree line when they heard someone approaching their position from behind. Jansen grabbed his M1 Carbine and turned toward the noise while Harrison kept his eyes forward towards the enemy.

It was Sergeant Parker approaching their position, "Okay fellas, the captain wants us at the very edge of the tree line when the Germans fall back into the city. So quietly move forward and find a position that offers you the best cover possible, but also you two need to have a wide field of view of the area between the woods and the city. And remember, don't shoot at the first Kraut that breaks out from the tree line. You want them to think it is safe, so they send a whole mess of those bastards across all at once. Then you open up on those Nazi assholes, understand?"

"Roger that," Harrison replied.

Parker moved away from the two men and retreated deeper into the woods as Jansen and Harrison inched their way forward until they found a position at the very edge of the tree line. Jansen got out his entrenching tool to create a small mound of dirt in front of their position to give the two a little more cover.

It was still a couple of hours before sunrise, the coldest part of the night. Jansen and Harrison were laying on the ground and trying not to shiver. Staying still was an important part of staying hidden. They could hear the fighting getting closer. Soon they could hear the voices of the German troops falling back as the Americans pushed forward through the woods between Scheuren and Bad Honnef.

Jansen and Harrison were watching the open area between the tree line and the edge of the city. From their position, Jansen and Harrison could see about 50 yards of the tree line. There was about a 20-yard gap between the trees and the first building.

At about 0530 hours Jansen watched as a German soldier emerged from the woods. He looked young, probably not even sixteen years old. The soldier's youth and inexperience were probably why he did not seem worried about walking out into the open. And from the Germans' perspective, the Americans they needed to worry about were attacking from the south.

124

Harrison watched as the German soldier passed into the city. He held his fire. Soon a few more Germans crossed the open area and made it safely to the city. Within a few minutes, a larger group of about twenty moved out from the protection of the trees and into the area between the woods and the buildings. Harrison took aim and opened fire on the nearest group of German soldiers.

Once Harrison began firing the whole company opened up and began firing on the Germans as they tried to retreat into the city of Bad Honnef. The first few seconds after the company started firing were the deadliest for the German forces. Jansen figured that Harrison by himself probably killed at least a half a dozen men as they tried to make the mad dash from the woods to the city.

Soon the men of Mike Company were linking up with men from the Second Battalion, trapping the Germans between the converging American forces. The Germans quickly set up a line of defense and began firing on Mike Company. Slowly the Germans were making their way into the city, but they were still taking heavy casualties. By 0600 hours the Germans were pushed back into the city of Bad Honnef.

After most of the German Army had made its way into the city, the German soldiers who had covered the retreat just surrendered to the Americans. Second Battalion was tasked to deal with the prisoners.

It was now time for the Americans to begin the assault on Bad Honnef. Sergeant Parker came over to Jansen and Harrison's position and told them which house they were assigned to attack.

Harrison began the attack by shooting at the house as the rest of the squad slowly advanced toward the house under his cover fire. Once they reached a position that offered them some cover, Harrison and Jansen moved forward to join the rest of their squad. They were now only about fifteen yards from the house. Harrison began firing on the house as the rest of the squad again advanced toward their objective.

Once the squad reached the house the Germans stopped returning fire, abandoned the house, and fell back farther into the city. Parker and his men entered the house and then gave the all-clear for Jansen and Harrison to advance. When they reached the house, Ellison met them at the door.

"Come on in guys," Ellison said as Jansen and Harrison approached the back of the house. "The Germans must have left when they saw us coming," he said lightheartedly.

Jansen walked into the house, most of the men of his squad were sitting or lying down on various pieces of furniture. A few were at the windows making sure that the Germans were not planning a counterattack to try and retake the house. But given how easily they had surrendered their position, the chances of a German counterattack seemed unlikely.

"We will hold here until we hear from Collins," Parker said.

Jansen found a place on the floor to sit down. Harrison sat down next to him, "Are you ready to switch off carrying the Browning?" Harrison said as he placed the machine gun on the ground and sat down on the floor with Jansen.

Jansen was cold, tired, and hungry. He let out a sign, trying not to think about how tired he was, finally he said, "Yeah, sure, I'll carry it for a while." Jansen took the satchels of ammo from his shoulders and handed them off to Harrison.

"Thanks," Harrison said, "I don't think marching slow makes carrying that thing any easier, but good job lugging it on that march to Meckenheim yesterday."

Jansen's mind returned to the march the previous day after they had been strafed by the Stuka dive bombers. That seemed like a lifetime ago, but it had been less than 24 hours. Jansen remembered how tired he was after that march, and now, almost a day later, his body was running on fumes. But the reality was that it didn't matter how tired he was, he and his fellow soldiers would have to push through being tired and fatigued because the Americans still had to continue to push the Germans north and out of Bad Honnef before they would get a break.

Jansen took off his helmet, leaned his head back against the wall, and closed his eyes, happy that he was in a house, and not lying on the cold ground. Parker came over, "Don't fall asleep Jansen, and put your helmet back on."

Jansen looked up at Parker, "Sure thing, sarge," he replied as he put on his helmet. Jansen was surprised that Parker had not peppered his instructions with some sort of insult, which was Parker's normal modus operandi when addressing Replacements.

Things were quiet for some time. Finally, Sergeant Collins entered the house, "Okay men, we are going to hold here for a while and give you men a chance to eat. We still don't have any normal supply lines, so getting Uncle Sam to feed you is not an option. You will have to 'liberate' some food if you want to eat anything. Just don't take too long, I am sure we will get orders to continue our advance into the city soon."

When Collins used the word "liberate," he was using the term in a way that was common among American soldiers that were now fighting on German soil. Although the Allied troops had not looted much when they were fighting in countries that had been occupied by the Germans, things had changed once they passed over the border into Germany. The general attitude among the Allied soldiers was that the Germans had caused this war, and so the Allies felt justified in stealing from the German homes they occupied. And this attitude was not limited to food.

Collins left the men to scrounge some food in the house.

"I think I saw a chicken coop nearby as we approached the house," Ellison said, "I'll bet I can find us some eggs." He then left the house in search of food.

"Be careful, stay low, and don't get caught out in the open," Parker warned as Ellison left the house.

"Jansen, you go down into the root cellar and see what you can find," Parker ordered.

Jansen got up, "Harrison, can you watch the Browning as I go down into the cellar?"

"No problem, Jansen," Harrison replied.

Jansen found the door that led down to the cellar and made his way down the stairs. At the bottom of the stairs, he found shelves where the canning jars were located. Over half of them were empty, but he was able to find a few jars of pears and brought them upstairs. Ellison had returned with some eggs and one of the other men found some stale bread.

When they were looking through the kitchen the men also found a can with about a pint of bacon grease in it, someone decided to fry the bread in the grease to make the stale bread more palatable. Jansen remembered that his mom would fry bread in bacon grease for him when he was a boy. His family called it "cracklins." For a moment Jansen's mind was transported back to simpler times.

Before long, the eggs had been boiled, the jars of pears had been opened, and the bread had been fried. Jansen looked at the food that was in his mess kit; three boiled eggs, half a jar of canned pears, and four small pieces of fried bread. The house got quiet as the men sat down to the first warm meal they had eaten in days.

Jansen took a bite of boiled egg, then took the rest of the egg and mashed it onto a piece of fried bread. As he sat there eating his "breakfast," Jansen was amazed how much better it made him feel. It was amazing how much better a man can feel after getting something as simple as a warm meal. Jansen finished up his breakfast along with the rest of the squad. He packed up his mess kit, grabbed the Browning machine gun, and looked for a place to sit and relax while they waited for Collins to come back and tell them to move out.

Jansen lit a cigarette and leaned up against the wall of the house. The men were enjoying their short break as they waited for orders. Jansen was grateful for the food and a little rest. He was still tired but getting out of the cold night air and eating a little warm food helped immensely. Jansen was not able to enjoy the break for long. Within a few minutes after the men had finished eating, Collins came into the house with their orders.

Collins found a place to sit and then began briefing the squad, "Okay men, Captain Horn needs us to push north on this street. Bad Honnef is a much bigger city than Erpel, Unkel, or Scheuren, so we expect that this will be some of the hardest fighting we've seen so far. We will have to coordinate our advance with the other units of the regiment so that means we can't let ourselves get too far ahead or behind from the other companies that are on either side of us. I guess that there is going to be a lot of waiting and holding our position as we wait for other companies to advance. We are going to form two columns on either side of this street and push north. We don't know how far the Germans have pulled back, but it seems like they have left the immediate area. Hopefully, in the first bit of our drive, we won't see too much action. The rest of the company is forming up outside, I need you to join them."

Jansen stowed his gear and grabbed the machine gun while the rest of his squad quickly grabbed their things and began working their way outside onto the street to join the rest of the company. It was just before dawn and the sky was beginning to lighten up to the east. Jansen was part of the column on the west side of the street. From there he could see the eastern skies above the German hills slowly growing lighter.

The men were given the order to move out. Jansen set up outside the entrance into the first house they cleared on the west side of the street. The home was empty, so it only took the men a few minutes to clear the building. As the men of Mike Company prepared to move farther down the street, Jansen could see the sun rising over the hills to the east of the city.

When the sunlight hit him, it almost made him feel colder than he was before. It was like the sunlight was tricking his body into thinking that it would get warmer, but the air was just as cold as it had been before. Jansen's body shivered for a second in protest as he and Harrison continued to move down the wide streets of Bad Honnef.

Mike Company progressed steadily through their sector of Bad Honnef for about an hour, then the men, along with the rest of their regiment, met heavy German resistance. Jansen wondered if this was because the 600 reinforcements had finally arrived to help repel the American advance.

Sometimes Mike Company was forced to wait for other units that were bogged down. Sometimes Jansen's unit was stopped by fierce German fighting. Bad Honnef was just a much bigger city than the three relatively small towns that Mike Company had already fought their way through.

As the day grew lighter, the danger for the Americans grew as well because it became more difficult to hide from enemy fire. One thing that helped the Americans was the fact that most of the homes in Bad Honnef were more spread out, not as tightly packed as they had been in the smaller towns the men had already passed through.

Also, there were plenty of trees and planter boxes in the city, giving the soldiers more places to hide and take cover as they advanced north.

It was now about 1130 hours, Jansen and Harrison had been trading off carrying the machine gun all morning. At this point, Jansen was carrying the Browning. The two men were set up behind a planter box, Jansen was firing on a group of Germans that were returning fire from a building about a hundred yards away, while the rest of his squad was trying to encircle the German position. At this point the Germans in Bad Honnef were in full retreat, trying to get as many of their men out of the city as quickly as possible. The Americans, at this point, were trying to make sure that they captured or killed as many of the retreating Germans.

Harrison tapped Jansen on the shoulder, Jansen stopped firing so that he could hear what his fellow machine gunner had to say. "I think the rest of the company has taken out the German position down the street. We can move closer to the house and get in a better position," Harrison told Jansen.

"Roger that," Jansen replied.

Jansen grabbed the machine gun and the two men moved further down the street and found a position that offered some cover. Jansen set up the machine gun and began firing on the German-held house.

Jansen could see Parker taking two groups of men and encircling the house. They were going to enter the house from the back forcing the Germans that hadn't already left to either surrender or go out the front door into the crosshairs of Jansen's machine gun.

Once Jansen could see that the rest of his squad had made it around the back of the house, he slowly stopped shooting. After a few moments, the front door opened, and a German soldier bolted out and onto the street in an obvious attempt to escape Parker's men who had just entered the back of the house.

Jansen aimed for center mass and fired. Jansen could see the bullets ripping into the man's torso and the spray of blood as the bullets exited the German soldier's back. The Nazi soldier was already dead when his body hit the cobblestone street in front of the house.

Jansen could see that the rest of the soldiers inside the house had realized that they were trapped and were surrendering to Sergeant Parker and the rest of his squad. Soon Jansen could see three German prisoners being marched out the front of the house.

As Parker's squad was taking this house, the rest of the battalion had been pushing the Germans out of the city and now the front lines were a few hundred yards farther north from their position.

Jansen and Harrison rejoined the rest of the squad in front of the house they had just captured. Parker ordered two of his men to take the prisoners to the rear.

"The rest of us will hold up here until we can find out what the old man wants us to do," Parker said to the remaining members of his squad.

Jansen could see Collins approaching their squad. Collins walked up to the house and spoke to his men, "Okay, I just heard from Captain Horn that we are supposed to hold our position here, it shouldn't be much longer before the Germans are completely pushed out of the city. Good work today men. Take a break, you've earned it."

"That house we just cleared seemed pretty nice inside, we'll just hold up in there," Parker told Collins.

As the men began to enter the house, Collins told his men, "It is almost noon, take this chance to liberate any food you can find and eat lunch."

As Jansen entered the house, he noticed that the Germans started a fire in the stove and that the house was noticeably warm. Jansen found a nice comfortable chair to sit in. He placed the Browning on the floor next to the chair and sat down. From the corner of his eye, he could see Sergeant Parker coming towards him. Jansen figured that Parker was going to yell at him for sitting or not giving up his seat to one of the Veterans. Jansen leaned forward, preparing to gather up his gear and move as Parker approached.

"Just relax for a bit Jansen, you've earned it. Nice work out there today," was all that Parker had to say.

Jansen leaned back into the chair's cushions and lit a cigarette. Outside on the outskirts of town, the last of the Germans soldiers were being driven out of the town of Bad Honnef.

CHAPTER THIRTEEN

WERWOLF

March 9, 1945
1157 Hours

"Okay men let's 'liberate' some food," Parker said to his squad as the men were relaxing on the various items of furniture in the German house. The soldiers got up slowly and began searching the house for food.

While the men were scrounging through the house, Sergeant Collins walked in and told Parker that now that the Germans had been pushed out of Bad Honnef, Captain Horn had decided to give the men a short break to get some rest.

Jansen overheard Collins say to Parker, "We will meet up for an After-Action Review in the company HQ at 1800 hours. Horn has set up the company HQ in the red brick house three doors down to the north. Your men should be able to get at least four or five hours of sleep before then."

"Let's get moving," Parker called out to his men, "the longer it takes to get you idiots fed, the less time we will have to sleep before the After-Action Review." The soldiers quickly began rummaging through the house looking for anything they could find to eat, knowing that they would be able to sleep after they had been fed.

"I'm going to go out back and look to see if there is a chicken coop near here," Ellison said. "Maybe I can score us some more eggs to cook up for lunch."

Ellison exited the back of the house while the other members of the squad were looking for food and depositing what they had found on a table in the kitchen. The kitchen was in the back of the house and had a window that gave a view of the back yard. Jansen was in the kitchen facing the window looking for food. He could see Ellison making his way over to one of the neighboring yards when he heard the distinctive sound of a rifle firing. The sound came from the back of the house. Through the window, Jansen could see Ellison's body slump over.

Jansen quickly moved to the window and yelled, "Ellison's been hit!"

There was only one building that the shot could have come from. It looked like an old, abandoned warehouse. Jansen's eyes scanned the warehouse windows. He saw movement in one of the open windows on the second floor.

Harrison was nearby, "Don't go out there Jansen!" he yelled.

Parker ran quickly to the back of the house, "Did anyone see where the shot came from?"

Jansen pointed to the open window on the second floor of the warehouse, "The shot must have come from that open window," Jansen told Parker.

"Harrison, you get on the Browning. Jansen, you and I are going to rush that building before that Nazi asshole has a chance to escape," Parker ordered.

Parker and Jansen grabbed their rifles and exited the house and took cover behind two trees in the backyard. Harrison set up the machine gun behind the threshold of the back door. Jansen and Parker looked at the windows of the warehouse but could not see anything that would indicate where the shooter was currently lurking.

Meanwhile, some of the other men from the squad made their way out to Ellison to give him first aid.

Parker motioned to Jansen to move out. The two men ran to the door of the warehouse and flung the door open while staying away from the opening. They peeked into the warehouse, the two men did not see anything and rushed into the building.

The ground floor was a big, open, and empty space with a dirt floor. Parker located a set of stairs leading to the second floor and motioned for Jansen to follow him. When the two men reached the stairs, they could see a set of footprints leading up the stairs, but nothing to indicate that the man who shot Ellison had gone back down the stairs.

Parker started slowly and carefully to walk up the staircase with Jansen following. At the top of the stairs, Parker noticed a tripwire and pointed it out to Jansen. Parker and Jansen stepped over the wire and found that it was attached to a German potato masher grenade.

The second floor had a long hallway with a series of doors that probably led to offices. The building looked like it had not been occupied for some time.

Parker whispered to Jansen, "I think if we spring this booby trap it will draw the Kraut out. We just need to find some cover to get behind."

The two men looked around and found a large metal desk about ten yards away from the tripwire. Parker found a piece of telephone wire and attached it to the tripwire while Jansen ran the wire back to the desk. The two men slowly lowered the heavy desk on its side and took cover behind it. Parker grabbed the telephone wire and gave it a good pull. The two men waited, a few seconds later the German grenade exploded.

Jansen watched the hallway doors, slowly, one of the doors began to open. It was dark in the hallway, the figure in the doorway was backlit from the light coming into the room behind him. It was clear that he was carrying a rifle. Jansen and Parker opened fire. The German man fell to the floor.

Parker kept his rifle pointed at the man's head and walked over to the body. Jansen followed. He kicked the rifle out of reach from the German. The light from the open doorway landed on the man, Parker and Jansen got their first good look at him.

The German was wearing civilian clothes and looked to be about thirty years old. His rifle looked old and well used. The shots from Jansen and Parker had all hit their mark. The man was unconscious and bleeding out from five bullet holes in his chest. Jansen watched as the man's face lost all its color and turned from pink to ashen. The wounded man finally breathed his last, it was now clear that the German's life had ended.

Jansen walked over and picked up the German's rifle. As he examined it, he noticed something carved into the stock. It was a symbol. The symbol consisted of a vertical line with hooks at the end and it was crossed in the middle.

"Sergeant, do you know what this marking means?" Jansen said as he showed the symbol to Parker.

"Son of a bitch!" Parker exclaimed, "That is Nazi asshole is a Werwolf!"

Jansen did not understand what Parker was saying and asked, "What the hell are you talking about?"

Parker replied, "Don't look at me like I'm crazy. I'm not talking about a man that turns into a wolf, like in the movies. Werwolves are German military that pose as civilians so they can hide out behind our lines and then they try to take out as many Allied soldiers as possible."

"What do we do with the body?" Jansen asked.

"Just leave it here, eventually someone will come looking for him. Let the poor bastard that finds him deal with the body," Parker replied, "And if no one comes looking for him, this bastard can just sit here and rot for all I care."

Jansen led the way out of the warehouse, he was eager to get back to Ellison. He was worried about what was happening to his friend.

When Jansen and Parker returned to the house, Jansen could see that Ellison was laying on a stretcher on the floor of the house. O'Connor, the medic, was working on the injured soldier. As Jansen entered the room, O'Connor looked up at Jansen and shook his head slowly indicating that he didn't think Ellison would make it.

Jansen somberly approached his friend. Ellison had been shot just below the heart and the wound was bleeding profusely. Jansen looked at his friend's face and could see the same ashen color that he had just seen in the face of the dying German man.

"Hey buddy, how are you holding up?" Jansen said as he kneeled down beside Ellison.

Ellison's head turned slowly to look at Jansen, "Garret! Nice to see you."

A lump began to grow in Jansen's throat as he grabbed Tim Ellison's hand. Garret could feel that Tim's hand was cold, "You're gonna be okay, Tim. You just got to hold on, alright?"

"Thanks for that, but I know that I'm not going to make it," Tim said. His voice was getting weaker and Garret could feel that Tim's grip was getting weaker as well.

"Is there anything I can do for you?" Jansen asked, his voice cracking halfway through the question.

"Yeah, when all this is over, I want you to visit my parents. I want you to tell them about my time here. Can you do that for me?" Tim said as he slowly closed his eyes.

A tear rolled down Garret's cheek. Garret took a deep breath in an attempt to clear the lump in his throat, "I'll visit your folks, I promise," he said.

"Thanks, buddy," Tim said to Garret as he let out his last breath. Garret took Tim's hand and placed it on his friend's chest.

Jansen looked up. All the men of the squad were looking at him in silence. Jansen looked down at his hands. He grabbed his injured hand and looked at the dirty old dressing that was covering the stitches he had gotten a couple of days earlier.

"Hey doc, do you have any fresh bandages for my hand?" he asked.

O'Connor reached into his bag and handed Jansen some bandages, "Here you go. Are you okay?" the medic asked.

"Yeah, I am just going to clean up and change the dressing on my hand," Jansen replied as he took the bandages from O'Connor.

Jansen slowly rose to his feet. He made his way into the bathroom that was just down the hall. Once Jansen was alone in the bathroom with the door closed, a wave of emotion and grief washed over him. He set down his rifle and walked over to the sink and began unwrapping the bandages on his hand. Jansen was trying not to sob as tears flowed down his face and onto his bandaged hand. He finished removing the dirty bandages and let them fall to the floor.

He stared at his wounded hand and could see that it was beginning to heal. Jansen took a deep breath and let out a heavy sign. He turned on the faucet and washed the dirt off his hands. Jansen then splashed some water on his face. He watched as the dirt of the past two days dripped off his face and his hands and into the sink.

Jansen took the clean dressing that O'Connor had given him and slowly wrapped the bandage around his injured hand. Jansen looked at himself in the mirror. He looked tired. His body was screaming for a rest. He opened the door and walked down the hall and into the main part of the house.

As Jansen rejoined his fellow soldiers, he could see two men carrying out the stretcher with Ellison's body on it. The men carrying the stretcher paused as Jansen walked up to them.

Jansen placed his hand on his friend's shoulder. Jansen took a deep breath and said in a labored tone, "Goodbye my friend."

Jansen watched as his friend was carried out of the house. Time seemed to slow down as the events of his friend's death washed over him like a flood. He was not overcome with emotion, he just felt nothing. No sadness, no anger. He just felt empty, like he was in another world. Jansen took a deep breath and looked up.

The rest of his squad just stood there for a moment. Then Parker spoke up, "Those damn Nazis! We had taken the city! Ellison didn't do anything wrong, just he was walking into a secured area."

Several of the men nodded in agreement.

"I still need to get you ladies fed," Parker said after a while to break the silence, "So, I need you to continue to look for food."

Some of the men had already collected some food and placed it on a table in the kitchen. Jansen found some summer sausage and some cheese and placed those items on the table as well. Harrison went down into the root cellar and brought up some canned peaches and several bottles of hard apple cider.

Soon the men were standing around a table that was loaded with bread, butter, sausage, cheese, canned fruit, and cider. Jansen got out his mess kit and was waiting for the Veterans to grab what they wanted before he took anything to eat.

Sergeant Parker saw Jansen standing silently, "I know you probably don't feel much like eating right now, but you will sleep better on a full stomach. Grab something before it's all gone."

Jansen paused for a second and then grabbed a couple of pieces of bread, sliced off some summer sausage and cheese, and went off to eat by himself now that he was the only Replacement in his squad.

Harrison called over to Jansen, "Hey, Jansen, sit with us. Now is not the best time for you to be alone."

Jansen could see the rest of his squad sitting down at the small kitchen table. Jansen took his food and joined the group.

"So, Jansen, where are you from?" Parker asked as Jansen sat down with the rest of the men.

"South Dakota," Jansen answered.

"Don't feel bad, we can't all be lucky enough to be from New York," Parker quipped.

After that, the men settled into eating the food they had 'liberated' and began telling stories about their lives back home in the states. Jansen was not very talkative under ideal conditions and now he was even less inclined to talk. He was content just to enjoy his food with a group of men he was just getting to know. He entered into the conversation occasionally, especially when the squad began talking about Ellison. Although most of the men at the table had not gotten to know Ellison very well, they all agreed that he was a decent soldier, which was high praise from the Veterans for a Replacement. They also agreed that he was generally a good guy, and he was fun to be around. Jansen thought that if you had to boil down Ellison's personality to one sentence that was a pretty accurate description of him.

It did not take long for the men to finish their meal. They were hungry, tired, and eager to get some rest. This combined with the fact that life in the Army had trained them to eat quickly, meant the men completed their meal in record time.

After eating, the men began looking for places to sleep. The house they were in was quite large and as luck would have it, there were enough beds in the house so that every man of Parker's squad was able to find a mattress to sleep on.

Jansen found a small room on the second floor with a small bed in it. It was now almost 1300 hours and Jansen's body was screaming for rest as he entered a bedroom on the second floor. At this point, Jansen had been awake for over 34 hours and had traveled over 23 miles both by truck and on foot.

Jansen walked into the room and closed the door behind him. He leaned his M1 Carbine against the wall next to the bed. Luckily, he did not have to worry about keeping track of the Browning machine gun while he slept because Harrison had decided to keep it after Parker and Jansen had taken out the sniper that killed Ellison.

There was not much in the room; just the bed, a chair, and a small dresser. The room had a small window with no curtains. The dim light of the March day filtered into the small room. There was a chill in the room, probably because it was so far away from the main living area of the house. But for all its faults, it was better than sleeping on the ground, and for that, Jansen was thankful.

Jansen walked over to the chair, took off his web gear, and laid it on the floor. He then sat down and began to take off his boots. He tried to forget about all that had happened recently and in the last couple of days. He just wanted to get some rest and knew that dwelling on past events he had no control over would not help him get the sleep his body longed for.

Jansen looked over at the bed, there were only a pillow and a couple of blankets on the bed. Jansen thought that was just as well that the bed did not have sheets since he was planning on sleeping in his uniform. Jansen took off most of his outer clothes like his field jacket and then removed his belt. He sat down on the mattress and then grabbed his rifle and cleared it. As he laid down on the mattress, he laid his rifle next to his body as he covered his body with the blankets.

Jansen laid his head back on his pillow and closed his eyes. For a moment, his thoughts turned to the loss of his friend, and a wave of grief washed over him. But in an instant, that grief was gone and was replaced with sheer exhaustion. Seconds later, Jansen fell asleep.

CHAPTER FOURTEEN

ITTENBACH

March 16, 1945
0800 Hours

There was a knock at the door. "Private Jansen, time to get up," a voice called out from the other side of the door.

"Thank you," Jansen said as he lifted his head from the pillow and looked around the small room. Everything in the room was just as he had left it before he went to sleep. The sun was coming in from the window. Jansen felt rested and warm, which had not been a common experience for the young soldier recently.

Jansen could easily say that at this moment in time that he was truly comfortable as he lay in a warm bed and on soft sheets for the first time in weeks. The air in the room was beginning to warm up as Jansen pulled himself out of bed. He winced a little as his bare feet hit the cold floor.

Jansen looked over at his dress uniform that was hanging on the wall of the bedroom. He pulled on his pants and stepped out into the hallway of the hotel. Jansen walked down the hallway to an open door that led to the bathroom.

Growing up on a farm in South Dakota during the Great Depression, he was not used to taking hot showers or even having an indoor bathroom. And even though his access to showers became a more common occurrence since he had been drafted into the Army, a hot private shower was still something of a novelty for this unassuming farm boy.

Jansen undressed and got in the shower. He placed his head under the showerhead. The warm water felt good as it ran through his thick dark hair. This was the first real shower he had taken in over a week. As the water washed over his body, it felt as though all the dirt and pain of the last few weeks were being washed away as well.

As he stood in the shower, with the warm water running down his back, it seems as though the water was washing away the tension he was feeling as well. Living in a state of heightened awareness that comes from being in combat was an almost constant part of his life since he had landed in the ETO. But, for this brief moment in time, that tension was washed away in a stream of warm water.

Jansen looked down at his hand. Doc O'Connor had removed the stitches a few days ago and Jansen could see that the wound had healed quite nicely. Jansen was surprised that the wound had healed so well considering all he had been through. He concluded that time and a little bit of care were all that was needed for any wound to heal properly.

Jansen got out of the shower, dried off and got dressed. He took out his shaving kit. Since the incident with Lieutenant Wilson, he always kept his shaving kit with him. He removed his razor and began to shave. This time he was able to make it through the process without cutting himself. It probably helped that now he was using a sink with warm water to shave and was not using his helmet filled with cold water in the middle of a street in a combat zone.

Jansen finished up in the bathroom and returned to his room. Jansen put his shaving kit into his duffle bag and put on his dress uniform. Jansen grabbed a folded piece of paper that was sitting on the dresser in the room. Jansen took the paper and shoved it into the breast pocket of his Eisenhower jacket. Jansen then went down to the first floor of the hotel to eat breakfast.

The hotel had a small serving room for its guests. The room was rather empty, only a few of the tables were occupied. Jansen was about to see if he could find a small table where he could eat his breakfast by himself when he heard a familiar voice call out to him.

"Private Jansen, come over here," an officer called out to him from a corner of the room. It was Chaplain Martin, "Have a seat, Garret, you look hungry."

Jansen walked over to the chaplain's table and sat down.

"Good morning Garret," Martin said, "did you sleep well?"

"Yes sir, it was nice to sleep in a warm bed for a change," Jansen replied.

"I guess it beats sleeping in a foxhole," Martin said, "There wasn't much choice for breakfast, so I just ordered for both of us."

"Thank you, sir."

"I am glad you were able to come here today. How are you holding up?" Martin asked.

"I'm doing well. I'm not sure I'm ready for this though," Jansen replied.

"You'll be fine, there won't be a lot of people. Besides, if you ever decide to become a pastor like yours truly, you will have to get used to speaking in front of people," Martin joked.

"Yeah, I don't think that will ever happen," Jansen replied wondering if the chaplain was just trying to be funny, or if he was being somewhat serious.

"It was so providential to run into you after chapel services last Sunday. I am glad you were able to make it. And thanks for telling me about Ellison. From what you said, it sounds like was a good guy," Martin said as he took a drink of coffee.

"Ellison was a good guy and a good friend. Now I know why the Veterans didn't want to get to know the Replacements, it hurts like hell to watch someone die that you have gotten to know," Jansen said.

"That is why I was so glad that you came and talked to me after chapel last Sunday. Losing a friend is never easy and it is always helpful to have someone to help you through it. I am glad I was able to help you with that."

143

A German waitress came by with a cup of coffee for Jansen. She looked tired like she had gotten up early and had already had a terribly busy day. Even so, Jansen thought that she was quite pretty. She had short light brown hair, a slender figure, and a simple, natural beauty about her.

"You want coffee?" she said in broken heavily accented English.

Jansen replied in German that he would. The waitress looked surprised and asked Jansen if he spoke German. Jansen told her in his limited German that he spoke Dutch but could speak a little German.

Martin looked at Jansen with a newfound respect, "So you speak German?" he asked.

"Not much sir, I grew up speaking Dutch, so it has been easy for me to pick up German because the two languages are so similar. And since I've joined the unit, we have taken thousands of German prisoners, so I have had a lot of experience talking to Nazi soldiers," Jansen replied.

Martin was impressed with this unassuming and remarkable young man, "Well soldier, you are full of surprises, aren't you?"

Jansen did not know how to respond. Finally, after a short but awkward pause, he said, "I guess so sir."

It was not long before the waitress brought breakfast over to Jansen and Martin's table. Both men were given a plate with German pancakes, bacon, and a couple of boiled eggs. Along with the two plates, she also brought a basket of rolls and placed them on the table as well.

"Do you mind if I say grace?" Martin asked Jansen.

"No sir, go ahead."

Chaplain Martin and Jansen bowed their heads. Martin prayed, "Dear Lord, thank you for this food that you have provided. And thank you for keeping Private Jansen safe in this incredibly dangerous time. We ask for your blessing on this food, and we ask you to bless the service we are about to perform for our fallen friend. Amen."

The two men began eating their breakfast. Martin took a bite out of a piece of bacon and asked, "Were you able to write down something that you could read for Ellison's eulogy?"

"Yes, sir. I hope it is okay. Would you like to look it over?" Jansen asked.

"You know you really don't have to call me 'sir,'" Martin said.

"I know, but it is just a habit," Jansen replied.

"I don't need to know what you wrote, I trust it is fine. But I would be happy to look it over if you think that would help."

"It would make me feel better if you told me what you think about it, sir," Jansen said as he took out the folded piece of paper from the breast pocket of his jacket and handed it to the chaplain.

The two sat in silence while they ate and as Chaplain Martin looked over the eulogy Jansen had written for Ellison.

Martin finished reading over the eulogy and said, "I think it looks good, Garret. It is a fine tribute to your friend," and handed the paper back to Jansen.

The two men finished their breakfast and made their way to the outside of the hotel. The morning air was crisp and clear. Jansen lit a cigarette as they walked out into the morning sunlight. As they walked over to where the chaplain's jeep was parked, Chaplain Martin began to tell Jansen about what was going to happen when they got to the cemetery.

"When we get there, I am going to make some last-minute arrangements with the honor guard for the funeral. All the services will be short because sadly, Ellison is not the only soldier being buried today. Just stay with me and I will tell you when Ellison's funeral is about to begin. At the start of the funeral, I will say a few words, then I will call you up to give the eulogy. Then will be the rifle volley which will be followed by the bugler playing *Taps*. Finally, the honor guard will fold the flag. I will have you accept the flag in place of Ellison's family. After the service, you can hand the flag off to me and I will make arrangements for the flag to be delivered to his family."

"I don't know if I'm ready for this, chaplain," Jansen said quietly as the two finally walked up to the jeep.

"Don't worry Garret, I know you'll do fine," Martin assured him as the two men climbed into the vehicle.

Chaplain Martin started the engine and gently pulled away from the hotel and drove through the town of Ittenbach. The cold morning air seemed to cut right through Jansen's uniform as the two men drove to the cemetery at the edge of town. As they made it to the edge of Ittenbach, the jeep drove into a wooded area. The shade of the trees made the morning seem colder than it had before.

Soon the two arrived at the cemetery. Jansen waited by the jeep and finished his cigarette as Chaplain Martin left to make the necessary arrangements with the commander of the honor guard detail. The sun was just beginning to peek through the tops of the trees. The grass in the cemetery was wet with dew. Jansen rubbed his cold hands to warm them after the jeep ride.

Soon Chaplain Martin returned, "As it turns out, I only have two funerals to do this morning. Ellison's funeral will be second. The first funeral will be in about half an hour, and Ellison's funeral will be right after that. Just stay with me through the first funeral, and that will give you a general feel of what to expect at Ellison's funeral."

"I'll just stay here in the jeep until then sir," Jansen replied.

"That's fine Garret. I just have a few more things to work out and then I'll join you," Martin said.

"Yes sir."

At that, Martin walked off to talk with some of the other chaplains that were also there to help officiate some of the funerals that were happening that day.

Jansen sat down in the jeep and pulled out his pocket Bible and began flipping through it. He had not had much of a chance to read it since Chaplain Martin had given it to him. His unit had been in combat almost constantly since he had received it a week and a half ago. But there had been some lulls in fighting when Jansen felt it was safe to get out the Bible and do some reading. There was even a time when Parker had caught Jansen reading his Bible and didn't say anything, contrary to the threat Parker had made to Jansen on the day he first received the Bible.

The sun was rising, and Jansen's body was washed in the late winter sunshine. Jansen looked up from his reading to admire the beauty and serenity of the area. The fighting on the front lines that had been such a huge part of Jansen's life for so long seemed so far away from him at this moment in time.

The cemetery was surrounded by trees and Jansen found the location to be quite beautiful and peaceful. The color of the evergreen trees shone brightly in the morning sun and contrasted beautifully against a cloudless deep blue winter sky. The organized rows of crosses marking the graves of fallen soldiers of previous wars stood as a reminder of the purpose of this place and showed a simple ordered beauty in their own way.

Soon Chaplain Martin returned, and the two men chatted briefly until Martin was called to officiate his first funeral. Jansen and Martin walked over to the burial site. Jansen took a place with a small group of soldiers that were at the gravesite. Jansen wondered who these other soldiers were and why they were there. He figured that they were probably support staff from the morgue detachment.

Jansen watched as Chaplain Martin conducted the funeral service. Jansen remembered back to when he first met Martin and how he liked Martin's simple easy-going style. Jansen could see that same calm demeanor in Martin as he conducted this service. As his message ended, Martin called the men to attention. This was followed by the rifle volley and the playing of *Taps*. Afterward, the flag was folded and handed off to one of the soldiers that attended the service. Jansen decided that the soldier was probably a friend of the man who was being buried.

After the funeral, Martin came over to Jansen, "Hello Garret, we need to go over to Ellison's gravesite now."

The two men walked in silence over to where Ellison's casket was laid. This was the first time Jansen noticed his friend's flag-draped coffin. Martin could sense that he should just remain silent and let Jansen process the gravity of the moment.

As the honor guard moved into position for Ellison's funeral, Jansen and Martin just stood there quietly. The honor guard consisted of ten men, seven men with rifles to fire the rifle volley, two men to fold the flag, and one bugler. You could tell that the honor guard had done this before. There was a detached mechanical nature in which they prepared for the funeral. As Jansen watched the ten men get into place, he realized that their perceived indifference to the ceremony did not come from a lack of respect for Ellison, but was instead because these men had done this so many times, that the weight of what they were doing was beginning to lose its meaning for them.

Finally, all the men were in position and the commander of the honor guard came over to Chaplain Martin, "We're ready to start whenever you are padre."

"Thank you, Captain, tell your men that we will begin shortly," Martin said then turned to Jansen, "It's time. I've seen what you wrote about Ellison. You'll do great."

Martin walked over to the head of the flag-draped coffin. The men present immediately stopped talking and looked at the young Army chaplain.

Martin cleared his voice and began to speak, "We are gathered here today to honor the life of Private Timothy Ellison and the ultimate sacrifice he made for his country. We know that Tim will be missed by his family and friends back home and also by the men he served with. Tim was born in Kansas to Jim and Edna Ellison. His family were farmers who lost their farm during the Depression, at which time Tim's dad moved his family to California to start a new life. Tim graduated high school and soon afterward was drafted into the Army. Those who knew Tim said that he had a good sense of humor and that he loved to tell stories. He was also seen as a good soldier by the men of his unit. By all accounts, he was a good man with hopes and dreams for the future. This makes his passing even more tragic. Today we return his physical body to the dust from which it came, and we commend his immortal soul to the Heavens. And as we do so we are comforted in our loss by the hope we have in a loving and merciful God, both in this life and in the life to come. Let us pray."

Jansen and the rest of the people present bowed their heads in prayer.

Martin continued, "Dear Lord, we commend the body of Timothy Ellison to your care. We pray for your comfort and strength for the family and friends he left behind. May your hand of peace and love be stretched out over those individuals who have lost Tim as part of their lives. Amen."

Jansen opened his eyes. Chaplain Martin looked at him and motioned for Jansen to join him by Ellison's coffin. As Jansen

CROSSING OVER AT REMAGEN

walked to where Chaplain Martin was standing, Martin said, "And now we will hear from one of Ellison's friends, Private Garret Jansen. Garret and Tim served together in Mike Company of the 311th Infantry Regiment."

As Garret made his way to where Chaplain Martin was standing, Martin whispered to Jansen, "I'll be right behind you if you need any help, but I know you'll do great."

Chaplain Martin took a step back. Garret removed the piece of paper that contained Tim Ellison's eulogy from his breast pocket. He cleared his voice and began to read what he had prepared.

"I hope that what I have to say will honor the memory of my friend, Tim Ellison, who died during the Battle of Remagen. I have been nervous thinking about what I have to say today as we bury my friend. In the end, all I can do is tell you all what it was like to know Tim and to be his friend. I first met Tim in the back of a deuce-and-a-half as we were being transferred to Mike Company. There were about ten of us on that truck, and at the time I didn't know that Ellison and I would be assigned to the same squad. But one thing I did know, and that was that Tim was a fun guy to be around. I am glad we ended up in the same squad and grateful that we became friends. Anyone who knew Tim knew that he loved to tell stories. I learned so much about his family and life back home because whenever he got the chance, he would have a story to share that not only communicated mundane facts about his life in California but in a way that told you a lot about Tim himself. Even the Veterans in our unit that didn't get to know Tim very well seemed to get a kick out of listening to the funny way he talked about his life back home. My friendship with Tim made the transition to life in combat more bearable. I probably knew Tim as well as anyone even though we lost him to a sniper's bullet only two and a half weeks after the two of us joined Mike Company. Tim was killed, not because he did something brave or stupid, but because he was trying to do something nice for the rest of his squad. He was looking for food that he could share with the men he fought alongside. He was killed doing something for others. And that is how I think we should remember Tim, that he was selfless, a good soldier, and a good friend."

Jansen folded the paper we had been reading from and placed it in his pocket. Martin came forward and placed his hand on Jansen's shoulder and said, "Good job Garret."

Martin addressed the small gathering of soldiers at the gravesite, "And please come to attention and salute as we honor Private Ellison with a rifle volley and the playing of Taps."

The men came to attention and saluted as the honor guard's rifle team fired three volleys. Jansen stood there in the cold morning air as the sounds of the gunshots echoed out into the German hills. After the rifle volley, there was a short moment of silence before the bugler began to play *Taps*.

Jansen thought of the last moment he had with Tim before his death as the slow, sorrowful, notes of the song rang out into the air. A lump began to grow in Jansen's throat.

When the bugler had finished playing two men, a sergeant and a corporal, slowly walked over to the coffin. They carefully lifted the flag from Ellison's coffin and folded it. The sergeant walked over to Jansen and said, "On behalf of the President of the United States, the United States Army, and a grateful nation, please accept this flag as a symbol of our appreciation for your loved one's honorable and faithful service."

The sergeant solemnly placed the flag in Jansen's hand. Jansen then quietly walked over Ellison's casket, placed his hand on it, cleared his throat, and said, "Thanks for being my friend. I will talk to your mom and dad for you. I will tell them about your time here and let them know that you weren't alone when you died." Jansen's voice trailed off as he fought back tears, "I'll make sure that they know that you died among friends."

The men from the morgue detail came forward to lower the coffin into the grave as Chaplain Martin concluded the funeral. Jansen walked back to the chaplain's jeep and waited as Martin finished up talking with a couple of other officers before he was ready to take Jansen back to the hotel.

"You did great. I know it must have been hard for you to do that. But admit it, it wasn't that bad now, was it?" Martin said lightheartedly. Jansen chuckled.

"I guess not," Jansen said as he handed the chaplain the folded flag from Ellison's coffin. It had not been as hard as he thought it would be, but he was still glad that the eulogy for his friend was behind him.

"Well, I'm glad you did it. I think what you said was perfect. And it was a good way to say goodbye to your friend. Now let's get back to the hotel," Martin said as the two men climbed into the jeep.

The air was noticeably warmer than it had been earlier in the morning and Jansen did not remember being as cold on the jeep ride back to the hotel. The sun was sitting a little higher in the sky and the long morning shadows cast by the trees and buildings were getting shorter as the jeep drove through the streets of Ittenbach.

Jansen and Martin returned to the hotel. The two men returned to their rooms, grabbed their luggage, and checked out of the hotel. While in his room, Jansen changed out of his dress uniform and was now wearing his fatigues.

When they met outside, Jansen and Martin began loading their things into the back of the jeep.

Jansen turned to Martin and said, "Thank you Chaplain Martin for making me speak at Ellison's funeral. I am glad I was able to do that for him."

"I kind of knew that it would be important for you to say goodbye to your friend," Martin replied, "Sometimes taking the time to properly grieve the loss of someone close to you is the very thing you need to do to heal. Not that you forget about the loss mind you, but rather, it helps one to focus on what that person meant to you, and helps you to not just focus on the pain of losing them."

Jansen crawled into the jeep as Martin got in and started the engine. The jeep pulled away from the hotel in Ittenbach on its way back to the front lines. Jansen's brief respite from combat was coming to an end. It was time for the Veteran infantryman to return to his unit, to his brothers in arms. It was time for the Veteran to return to combat.

Appendix

Map showing the general route traveled by Jansen and his unit on March 8th & 9th, 1945. (Courtesy of Google Maps)

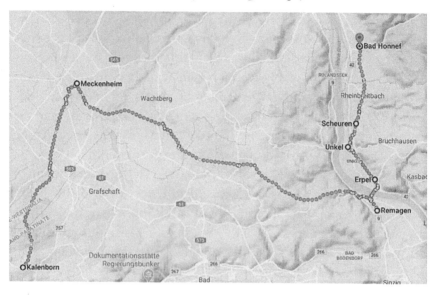

My dad (on the right), Corstian Klein, with some of his Army buddies in Germany.

ABOUT THE AUTHOR

Michael Klein lives in the Pacific Northwest with his family. Mike and his wife Rebecca have two children and one grandchild. Mike was born in Canada and raised in the United States. He has been a soldier in the U. S. Army, and an airman in the U. S. Air Force. Mike has worked as a teacher (having taught both in the U. S. and overseas), a banker, and currently works in the aerospace industry. This is his first novel. Mike has always had a desire to be an author. Mike's father Corstian was a church pastor, carpenter, and a prison ministry director. Mike's parents Corstian and Alice taught him from an early age to have a deep and abiding love for Jesus Christ. Mike's dad, Corstian, instilled in him the importance of hard work and service   to   others.